DREAM WANDERERS
The Escape

PAULA BROWN

A Mouse Gate™ Adventure

Mouse Gate™
1103 Middlecreek
Friendswood, Texas 77546
281-992-3131 TEL
www.MouseGate.com

Copyright © 2016 by: Paula Brown
All rights reserved
ISBN: 978-1-59095-791-2
UPC: 6-43977-77911-3
Library of Congress Control Number: 2016948331

Printed in the United States of America with simultaneous
printings in Australia, Canada, and United Kingdom.

FIRST EDITION
1   2   3   4   5   6   7   8   9   10

This is a work of fiction. The characters, names, events, views, and subject
matter of this book are either the author's imagination or are used fictitiously. Any
similarity or resemblance to any real people, real situations or actual events is purely
coincidental and not intended to portray any person, place, or event in a false,
disparaging or negative light.

To Tricia and Rob,
for making my dreams come true.

A special Thank You to my sister Nancy.
This wouldn't have been possible without you.

About the Author

Paula Brown is a freelance travel writer who also has a love for science fiction and Walt Disney World. Paula is the coauthor of *Dining at Walt Disney World: The Definitive Guide*. She is also a contributing author to *InsiderScoop® to Walt Disney World®* series of books. Other works of fiction include The *Coffee Cruiser* and *It's About Time*.

Paula lives in Florida with her husband and daughter.

About the Book

Dream Wanderers guide you through your worst nightmares. Far across the universe, an elite school runs a special program, training the Dream Wanderers of tomorrow.

But what happens when...

Gren and Lawson will soon achieve the impossible, becoming the first male/female partners to make it through the program. Or with they? Their feelings for each other and Lawson's disdain for an unbreakable rule, risk their expulsion.

They wander into a nightmare of their own...

When Lawson and Gren disappear, most assume they've run away together. But their four best friends aren't so sure. Following a shaky clue, they enlist the help of a crazy old man and set out to find the truth. Soon, the dream Wanderers will take on an entire army, as the fate of two worlds hangs in the balance.

Prologue

"Gren. Gren! Gretchen Ellen!"

"Huh? Oh, I'm sorry, Mom, I guess I was daydreaming." Gren hadn't really been daydreaming as much as she had been trying to not look at the boy who was standing in front of the T-shirts on the other side of Mickey's of Hollywood. He looked familiar to her but she couldn't place him anywhere. She wondered if maybe they went to the same school. She was in the accelerated program and there were a lot of people in her grade that she didn't know. She couldn't recall ever seeing him there but she knew that they had met before.

"Well, we are at the place where dreams come true, so daydreaming is to be expected." Gren's mother let out a small chuckle, pleased with her own joke. "I just heard a cast member mention that Winnie the Pooh is going to be out for pictures soon. We're going to walk over there so that your sister can get in line to meet her namesake. Tigger and Eeyore might be out as well."

Gren could not hide her disappointment. "I thought we were going to ride Rock 'n' Roller Coaster! The lines are shortest at the beginning of the day."

"Your father and I have been talking about that. Winnie is too young for a ride that intense, and quite honestly he and I don't want to ride it. Now that we're Disney Vacation Club members we'll be returning each year. Maybe you and Winnie can ride it next time."

"There's a single rider line," Gren said quickly. "I could ride by myself and meet you guys after Winnie gets her pictures."

Gren's parents exchanged a look. "Okay," her mother said at

last, "as long as the single line isn't too long. We'll meet you by the entrance to The Great Movie Ride in half an hour. That's behind the Sorcerer's Hat."

Taking a step towards gift shop's the door, Gren smiled. "I know. I'll be there."

Winnie, Gren's sister, stepped in front of her. "He is kind of cute."

"Who?" Gren asked, trying to get around her.

"The boy you were staring at. I bet he's about your age."

Gren rolled her eyes. "I don't know who you're talking about. And make sure that you smile in the picture this time! You know how poorly the one with Mickey turned out." Gren made it around her sister and walked through the door. She look back into the shop one more time. The boy was gone.

• ○ ◐●◐ ○ •

Even though it was early in the day Disney's Hollywood Studios was getting crowded. Hollywood Boulevard was already packed and Gren was sure that everyone was planning on riding Rock 'n' Roller Coaster first. As she turned the corner towards Sunset Boulevard she could see a flash of yellow in the distance. She assumed that it was Winnie the Pooh was out to sign autographs, take pictures, and give hugs. She was curious as to what other characters were out but she was in too big of a hurry. All she wanted to do was to get to Rock 'n' Roller Coaster. Something told her that she needed to ride it right away and she wasn't sure why.

When she made it to the ride's entrance she noticed that the line was already long. She was sure that she would not make it back to meet her family in time. As if out of nowhere, a cast member walked up to her. "I'm not supposed to do this," he said, "but I got a couple of magical FASTPASSES that are gonna go to waste. If the two of ya want them, they're yours."

"Thanks," a male voice answered. Gren had not realized that the young man that she has seen in the store was suddenly standing next to her. "We'll take them. Won't we?"

"I, um...," Gren stammered. She thought for a moment. "Wait...they don't use paper FASTPASSES anymore."

The cast member rolled his eyes. "That's why they call 'em 'magical'. They'll work. Trust me."

"I was going to get in the single rider line," the boy quickly said to Gren. "If you're not riding with anyone, we can ride together. With these 'magical' FASTPASSES it will go quicker."

"Okay," Gren said. She took one of the FASTPASSES and the boy took the other. There was something unusual about the ticket but she didn't know what. She had seen plenty of pictures of the old paper FASTPASSES and this didn't quite match. She glanced at the cast member's name tag. "Thanks, Roy."

"My pleasure," Roy said. "Just remember to hold on tight to those passes for a ride that ya won't soon forget."

As they walked towards the FastPass+ entrance Gren was not at all uncomfortable, which surprised her. There was something about the boy that totally put her at ease. She was about to ride one of the most extreme Disney rides with a boy that she had never met before, even though she couldn't shake the feeling that somehow they were already close friends.

"I'm Lawson," the boy said as they walked.

"I'm Gren." She started to hold out her hand but pulled back. For some unexplained reason she didn't want to shake his hand. Lawson didn't seem to notice.

"Is that short for Gretchen Ellen?" Lawson asked.

Gren was surprised and a little bit unsettled. "Yeah. I'm named after both of my grandmothers. How did you know?"

"I saw you in the gift shop a few minutes ago. Man, your mother is loud!" Embarrassed, Gren looked down didn't reply.

Lawson regretted the comment. "My parents were Star Wars fans, which is how I got my name."

Gren thought for a moment. "Lawson...as in Denis Lawson? The actor who played Wedge?"

"Wow, you're good. No one ever figures that out."

"My mom is slightly obsessed," Gren admitted. "We have to do everything that we can this morning because we're going to ride Star Tours all afternoon. She wants to hit all six planets. Maybe you could join us?" She was surprised by the invitation, partially because she was never that bold but mostly because it felt like spending time with Lawson was the most natural thing in the world.

"That would be fun, but I doubt that I'll be able to."

"Bring your parents along," Gren suggested. "You said that they're Star Wars fans."

Lawson glanced away, knowing that he was about to make Gren uncomfortable. "My parents died a few years ago. I'm here with a special group."

Gren was embarrassed. For some reason she wasn't surprised to hear that Lawson was an orphan. It was almost like she knew it as soon as she mentioned his parents. "I'm sorry."

"You didn't know." Lawson paused for a second. "Hey, I know this is going to sound weird, but have we ever met before? You look so familiar to me."

"I was wondering the same thing," Gren replied. "Where are you from?"

"I live here in Florida. How about you?"

"Massachusetts. This is my first trip to Florida."

"And I've never been to Massachusetts."

"Maybe ya saw each other in your dreams," someone said. Gren immediately realized that it was Roy. "Stranger thin's have happened. And I need to see the times on those magical FASTPASSES."

Gren and Lawson both showed Roy their tickets and moved forward in the line. "How did he get up here?" Gren whispered.

"I have no idea."

The FastPass+ line moved quickly. A minute or two later they were at the spot where the MagicBands are scanned. Both Gren and Lawson were surprised to see Roy for a third time. They tried to hand him their passes. "Keep 'em," Roy whispered. "Stick 'em in a pocket or somethin'. Whatever ya do, make sure that ya don't lose them. Ya both will need 'em for the ride of a lifetime."

"Thanks," Gren said as she started to walk again. She glanced back. She could only see the back of a cast member's head and it did not look like the same person. "That was strange," she said to Lawson.

"That he didn't take our passes?"

"That, and his name tag. It said 'Roy' and under that 'Abacu'. There was no state or even country listed."

Lawson thought for a moment. "Must be part of the College Program. Abacu University or something."

"Maybe, but isn't he a little bit old for that?"

° ° ° ⬤ ° ° °

A few minutes later Gren and Lawson were watching the video before the ride. Gren was a little bit nervous, she had never been on such a roller coaster before, but somehow knowing that she would be riding with her new friend made her feel more at ease. She was pretty sure that Lawson was nervous as well, but he was trying hard not to show it. The next thing they knew they were getting into a ride vehicle. They had been placed in the very last row. "Make sure ya keep your heads back," a someone said as he checked their harnesses. Gren glanced up and saw that it was Roy yet again. Ya got those magical FASTPASSES still?" he whispered.

"In our pockets,' Lawson replied.

"Good. The two of ya are in for one wild ride. Tell Sham that Roy said he needs to stop by sometime."

"Sham?" Gren repeated but it was too late, Roy was nowhere to be seen. The anticipation for the ride grew quickly. As the countdown started everything changed for Gren. What she thought was real blurred and she felt as if she was looking at her life through another person's eyes. Everything was different, as if she was someone else entirely. Even her memories were changing. The ride launched but Gren did not even notice.

The Learning Center's Covenant

As a Dream Wandering student at the Learning Center, I promise to take my gift seriously. I will use this gift only within the laws and regulations of Terra. I will spend time with my partner, knowing that this relationship is vital to my completion of the program. I will have no physical contact with students of the opposite gender. I will follow the rules of the Learning Center, knowing that those in charge know what is best for me.

Signature _____

Date _____

Chapter One

Lawson had been running for what felt like forever. The fire was gaining on him; there was no way he could outrun it. His only chance for survival was a small lake that he knew was somewhere in the vicinity. With a little bit of luck, the fire wouldn't be able to spread past the lake. His strength was fading; he wasn't sure he could make it. The fire was so hot he was certain the hair on the back of his neck had burned off.

"Follow the birds," a soft, comforting voice instructed. Although he heard Gren's voice, Lawson couldn't see her anywhere. He could feel her presence, urging him to go on. "The birds will show you the way to the lake." Lawson took just a moment to look up and saw a flock of orange and blue striped birds flying in formation. To follow them, he would have to backtrack a bit, right to the fire's edge, but Gren had never led him wrong in the past. He ran faster, trying hard to keep up with the birds and failing.

"Don't strive so hard. Just keep your eyes in their direction and you'll be there soon." Lawson took a deep breath and, ignoring Gren's advice, tried to run faster. He fell, ripping the shirt of his blue uniform on a burning bush. Gren gasped. "Are you okay?"

Lawson stood up and pulled on his sleeve, which was still caught in the bush. The sleeve ripped from his shirt and caught on fire. He brushed himself off. "I'm fine, but the birds are gone Which way do I go?" Gren's voice was calm once again. "The same direction. You're almost there."

Lawson started to run again, sure he was about to be consumed by the fire. He had twisted his ankle, but he wasn't about to admit how badly it hurt...not even to himself. He was suddenly at the top of a hill; at the bottom was the lake. He was going to make it! He started running even faster down the hill, tripped almost immediately, and rolled the rest of the way. He could hear Gren suppress a laugh. She'd have points marked off for that! At the bottom of the hill he tried to stand as gracefully as he could, brushing himself off a second time.

"Swim to the other side of the lake, and you'll be safe from the fire."

Lawson walked to the water's edge, bent down, and stuck his hand in. "The water's too cold. I'll die of hypothermia."

"No, the water's warm," Gren's voice told him. "Try it again."

Not believing her, he felt the water a second time. It was perfect. He waded into the lake. He glanced around, looking for Gren, even though he knew he wouldn't see her. He walked slowly, not realizing that the water became deep very quickly. Soon he was over his head.

"Swim!" Gren screamed. "You need to make it across to be safe!"

"I can't do it!" Lawson managed to say, fighting for each breath. "My strength is gone." He coughed twice, swallowing water each time. He felt as if he were about to go under.

"Use some of my strength." Gren's voice was calm again. "Do it for me."

Lawson started swimming; suddenly knowing he could make it across. There was no more water in his lungs, his ankle didn't hurt anymore, and he felt as if he could swim all rotation. Soon, he saw where the birds had landed on the other side. He made them his target; he'd follow the birds, as Gren had originally suggested.

In almost no time at all, he made it safely across the lake, the fire a distant memory. He climbed out of the water and lay on the beach, the nearby birds ignoring him. He breathed in the clear air and closed his eyes.

• ◦ ◐ ⬤ ◑ ◦ •

"There were several *major* mistakes. Who would like to go first? Lawson? It was your dream, I'll give you the first pick."

Lawson sat up and shook his head. He had only been awake for a few seconds; he didn't even know where to begin. He looked at Hutch, his teacher and mentor. "Can I have a micro to get the water out of my ears?"

"There's no water in your ears...it was a dream," Hutch reminded him. "No more stalling. You know as well as I do that it's best to talk about the dream while it's still fresh in your mind. Now, tell me a mistake."

"Gren laughed," Lawson said, glancing at his best friend with an apologetic look.

"You're right. Laughing isn't allowed." Hutch broke a smile. "I almost laughed, too; it *was* pretty funny watching you tumble down that hill." He became stern again. "People take having their dreams wandered *very* seriously. If they think you're laughing at them, you'll lose a client. Believe me, you'll see funnier things than Lawson rolling. You need to maintain you composure. Gren, tell me another mistake. A bigger one."

"I cared too much," Gren said quietly.

"Exactly!" Hutch almost screamed the word. "Clients will be depending on you to get them through their dreams. If you sound worried, they'll be worried, and it will only make their dreams worse. You need to be a smooth, calming voice to help them through their problems. I know you two are close...is it too hard for you to work together?"

"No," they said in unison.

"Good. I'd hate to be switching around partners this far into the program, but I will do it if I have to." Hutch took a drink from the mug in front of him. "It's been a long session, so I'll bring up my last point, which goes back to what Gren just said. You can't get personal. Gren, you gave some of your strength to Lawson. You told him to do it *for you*. That will work for you two, but not for a client. They don't know you *or* your strength."

Hutch started to pack up his equipment. "It was a good effort, both of you. You lost . . . ten points. Take the rest of the rotation off. I'll see you again the rotation after next. Lawson, it will be your turn to wander."

A unit later, Lawson and Gren sat under a yellow tree, enjoying its fruit. "That's the worst part," Lawson complained. "I hate having my dreams wandered. It's so embarrassing."

"At least it's just me. If Hutch decided we needed to switch partners . . ." Gren shuddered.

"I don't mind having *you* wander my dreams," Lawson said. "Not really. But it's hard knowing that Hutch is doing it too, even if he's just a silent observer. Do you think he ever wanders without our permission?"

Gren looked shocked. "That's against the law!"

"So what's time in a labor camp to a Dream Wanderer?" Lawson asked. "He could just wander everyone's dreams until they do what he wants them to. Have you ever thought about how much power we could have?"

"Shhh!" Gren glanced around to make sure no one was listening. "Talking like that will get us both thrown out of the program...and with only one orbit left. My parents would never forgive me! Besides, they'd remove the gift before throwing the *criminal* into the labor camp."

Lawson placed his hand right above Gren's, as close as possible without actually touching it. "Don't worry, I wouldn't really do it. It's just that sometimes the whole thing is so overwhelming."

"Have you given any more thought to what you're going to do after graduation?" Gren asked, changing the subject. "Where you might want to apprentice?" She carefully moved her hand away; if they were caught almost touching, there would be consequences, and Lawson was too close for comfort. She didn't know what the consequences were and didn't want to find out.

"I've thought about it a lot. I think maybe that's why my dreams have been full of danger lately. The fire represents not being able to go back, but I'm scared of going forward. Does that make any sense?"

Gren laughed. "We're supposed to help people get *through* their dreams, not interpret them. But I did learn one thing from your dream earlier."

"What's that?"

"You'll never be able to make it without me!" Gren picked a handful of grass and threw it playfully at Lawson. He did the same back at her, and the two of them were soon enjoying the fight.

Little did they know they were being watched.

Chapter Two

Few people on Terra cared much about their own galaxy. They lived happy, peaceful lives. Life on other planets was something for storytellers. It was also for dreamers, and so Dream Wanderers needed to know about the concept.

To Calli, that was one of the hardest things in the Learning Center. Her green uniform represented that she was in her second-to-last orbit before graduation. After that, she would be an apprentice for three orbits before becoming an official Dream Wanderer. Those in their final orbit no longer had to sit through the long, boring classes, like the one Calli sat through now, explaining the different things that might be found in dreams. The Blues had more practice and fewer practical lessons.

Calli glanced at Tayo, her new partner. Tayo was leaning against her arm, her eyes closed. Calli was sure Tayo was asleep. She considered briefly wandering into Tayo's dream and telling her to awake up, but if she was caught she'd be immediately expelled, the gift of dream wandering permanently removed from her soul. Instead, she gently nudged her partner, who woke with a start.

"Huh?" Tayo said sleepily.

"Shhh," Calli whispered. "You were asleep. I don't want to have to change partners again."

Tayo put her hand over her mouth to hide a yawn. "Sorry," she whispered back. "How much longer?"

"Not too much," Calli replied.

As if on cue Charla, the teacher of the front of the room, turned off the galaxy map and turned on the lights. "So you see,

Greens other planets, right here in our galaxy, are capable of sustaining human life. Some historians even believe that large ships filled with people left Terra thousands of orbits ago and colonized the planets Abacu and Eden. I personally doubt it.

"Now, I want each of you to come up with a plan for what you would do in a dream situation for someone who believes in life on other planets. You'll present it when we meet again, rotation after next. Greens, you're dismissed."

Later that rotation, Calli and Tayo sat in the dining area. Since they had just become partners, they spent as much time as possible together; being able to work well with your partner was one of the most important aspects of training. Calli was tired of changing partners. One by one, her four previous partners had been dismissed from the program. Tayo's luck hadn't been much better; she had watched three partners leave. It was unusual for anyone to make it through the entire program with the same partner, but three or four changes was excessive.

Calli and Tayo both noticed Lawson and Gren entering the room. If they graduated at the end of the orbit, they would be the first male/female partnering *ever* to make it through without a change. Usually a boy and a girl were partnered only as a last resort, but somehow, with these two, it worked.

"Mind if we sit here?" Gren held a tray of food, which she put on the table. She sat down and Lawson sat next to her. Still picking out their dinners were Titus and Sham, partnered Blues who were Lawson's roommates.

"The Partnering Ceremony is only four rotations away," Sham commented. "I can't believe we're in our last orbit!"

"Speak for yourself." Calli threw him a dirty look. She brushed her short, brown hair out of her eyes. Physical contact between genders was strictly prohibited, but if there was anyone she was *almost* willing to break that rule with, it was Sham. She tried hard not to think about it; one of her biggest fears was that Sham would pop up in a dream of hers that was being wandered.

"I don't see why they make the Partnering Ceremony such a big deal," Tayo added. "Nobody stays with the same partner as when they were Whites." Gren cleared her throat. "*Almost* nobody. I'll never understand how you two have made it together for so long."

"Me neither," Lawson teased, throwing a playful look at Gren.

"I almost requested to change partners," Gren said with a serious look on her face.

"When?" Calli asked.

Gren thought for a micro. "Let's see . . . first when we were Whites, then when we were Browns, then Purples . . ."

Lawson joined her. "Then Reds, then Oranges, then Yellows, then Greens, and finally in our last session with Hutch."

"You two are amazing," Titus remarked. "It's almost like you know each other's thoughts."

"I don't know her thoughts, but I know her dreams," Lawson joked.

"I thought that's what you were going to say," Gren added with a grin.

Later that same rotation, Gren, Calli, and Tayo sat in their dormitory room with Lanna and Macy, also partnered Blues. There was an unused bed in the corner; if Gren had a female partner, it would have been hers. It was unusual for Blues and Greens to share a room, but since Calli and Tayo had recently been partnered, the leader of the Learning Center made an exception to give them the chance to get to know each other, away from the other Greens.

So far, things seemed to be shaky for the new partners. Calli really enjoyed being with the older wandering students, even if they were only older by one color. It somehow made her feel more mature than her fifteen orbits. Tayo liked Gren. She wasn't thrilled with Lanna or Macy, and she didn't understand Calli's fascination with age. Their time would come soon enough.

"So what are you going to do?" Lanna asked Gren. It was a subject that at least one of her roommates seemed to bring up every few rotations. "What if your feelings for Lawson slip into one of your dreams?"

"What feelings for Lawson?" Gren asked innocently. "I've told you over and over again...we're just friends. That's all we can be if we want to stay in the program, and I'm happy with that."

"I bet after you graduate the two of you will become joined," Calli said.

"Joined?" Gren twirled her long, red hair around her finger. "Lawson and I aren't going to become joined. After we graduate we'll apprentice..."

"Together," Macy interrupted.

Gren ignored her. "And then we'll practice dream wandering somewhere. Together or separate, I don't know. Lawson has big plans. He'd like to travel, see more of Terra, maybe be a wandering Dream Wanderer!" She laughed at the joke, even though Lawson had told it to her so many times. "But I have my family to think about. I know they're not going to want me to go too far."

"Is that why Lawson spends his breaks with you?" Calli asked. "Because you want to be with your family, and he wants to be with you?"

Lanna and Macy each gave Calli a dirty look. "Lawson doesn't have any family of his own," Gren explained. "His parents were killed in an explosion right after he entered the program. That's why it means so much to him. They were incredibly proud to have their only child be a Dream Wandering student. And that's why he spends breaks with us. He's a ward of the Learning Center. He has no other place to go."

The room Lawson shared with Sham and Titus in the boys' dormitory was quite a bit smaller than the girls' quarters. There was an empty bed in the corner of their room, as well. "I hear the Greens were getting the 'life on other planets dream' lecture this rotation," Titus informed his roommates. "I sure don't miss those classes!"

"I don't know," Sham said. "Don't you think there could be life somewhere else out there?"

Lawson laughed. "No I don't. The whole idea is ridiculous. The chances are against it."

"I don't know," Sham repeated. "I know this guy, Roy, who claims he's from Abacu."

"Sounds like he needs *his* dreams wandered." Lawson grinned. "I'd be willing to do it for free . . . as soon as I get my license."

Chapter Three

There was no light anywhere, not even a spark. Gren knew she wasn't alone. She could hear it breathing; feel its breath on her neck. She knew it was big...a giant monster of some type. She stumbled in the dark, trying to get away.

"It's not big, and it's not dangerous," Lawson's voice told her.

"Yes it is!" Gren exclaimed. "It's huge...I just know it!"

"No, Gren. It's just a baby. Over your head there's a light. Turn it on, and you'll see how small it is."

Her hand shaking, Gren reached up and turned on the light. She wished that she had kept it off; in front of her was a gargantuan beast, twice as tall as she was. It had two heads, sharp yellow teeth, and enormous arms that were reaching right for her. The light shone strangely off its silver-gray fur. "I *knew* it wasn't a baby. How do I get out of here?" Gren's voice was filled with fear.

"The door is right behind you," Lawson said.

Panicking, Gren rushed out the door and closed it behind her, locking the monster inside. She breathed a sigh of relief as she turned around...only to stand face to face with two more of the hideous creatures. She started to run. "You can outrun them," Lawson's voice said calmly. "They're slow."

Gren ran as hard as she could, the monsters close behind. They weren't as slow as Lawson's voice had suggested, but she pushed herself harder because he told her to.

"You can make it," Lawson's voice said quietly. "Focus on that tree up ahead. Run to the tree, climb it, and you'll be rid of them."

Gren saw the tree; she was almost there. Once again she could feel monster breath on her neck. She made it to the tree and climbed. The creatures stayed on the ground, their long arms reaching for her. Gren climbed higher and higher until she was sure she was out of their reach. She reached the top of the tree; it swayed gently in the wind.

For the first time she looked down. To her horror, she realized that the tree was growing on the edge of a cliff. The wind picked up and grew stronger. "I'm going to fall!" she screamed.

"No, Gren, it's just a gentle breeze," Lawson said without much conviction. "A harmless, gentle breeze!"

"I'm going to fall!" She heard the crack, felt the branch she was on break very slowly. Suddenly she was falling.

Gren awoke with a start. "I *hate* dreams where I fall!" she said out loud, not really aware of the others in the room. She looked around to get her bearings. "Oh, I forgot where I was for a moment."

The look on Hutch's face was pure disappointment. "Lawson, what have I told you a thousand times? What rule is it that you seem to have such a hard time remembering?"

Lawson hung his head. "Don't call her by name."

"Exactly! It can have disastrous results. Look at what just happened here. Gren, was Lawson's presence in your dream a comfort or a distraction?"

"I wouldn't say a distraction," Gren said, trying to help her partner, "but it wasn't because he used my na..."

"Well it certainly wasn't a comfort," Hutch reminded her. "I know that you two are almost through the program, but last orbit or not, if you keep working like this you will *never* make Dream Wanderer. I'm not even going to grade this session, it was that bad."

Hutch relaxed a little. "We won't be meeting rotation after next because of the Partnering Ceremony. Enjoy the break, but keep studying. We'll meet again in four rotations."

. . ●◉● ● .

Gren followed Lawson as he hurried down by the lake. "Come on, Lawson, wait up," she called with frustration.

"Leave me alone," he muttered.

Gren refused to give up. "It's me. We talk about everything, remember?" She ran to catch up to him. "They're watching us right now, from the main building. I saw Charla in the window. If you don't stop and talk to me, I'll . . ."

"You'll what?"

"I'll touch you!" Gren almost screamed out the words. "Very obviously, so everyone will see it. Then we'll both have to suffer the consequences."

"Fine," Lawson replied. "In fact . . ." He stopped where he was and very deliberately reached for Gren.

"*No!*" Gren screamed and pulled away.

"It's a stupid rule, anyway," Lawson mumbled. "They partner us for over seven orbits, and we're not allowed to touch each other? Stupid."

Gren changed the subject. "So we had one lousy wandering session. It's not worth getting thrown out of the program."

"It's not the session," Lawson said slowly. He started to walk again.

"What?" Gren asked, trying to keep up. "You've always been able to tell me everything. Whatever it is, we'll get through it together."

Lawson stopped and sat down in the sand. He didn't care how dirty it made his blue uniform. He waited until Gren sat next to him. "I didn't get in."

"Get in where?" Gren asked.

"The apprenticeship program," he explained. "The one near where your family lives." He started to run his fingers through the coarse sand. "The one you've already been accepted to. The one we were going to join together."

"I never said I was actually going to go..."

"It's all you've ever wanted!" Lawson sighed. "And I understand. You want to be close to your family. I . . . I just want to be close to you. I know I shouldn't, but I do."

"Lawson, we can't think like that. If it ever showed up in one of our dreams, we'd be released from the program."

"They're the ones who threw us together!" Lawson immediately regretted raising his voice. "It's a cruel thing for them to do to us."

Gren tried to change the subject. "You've been accepted to two other apprenticeship programs. Will you take one of those?"

"Will you come with me?"

Gren looked away.

Lawson sighed. "You know me, Gren. I've always said I wanted to see more of Terra. Maybe I'll go as far away from here as I can." He laughed. "Or maybe I won't even become a licensed Dream Wanderer. Maybe I'll sell out my trade to the highest bidder, working on the Black Market and deliberately calling people by their names in their dreams."

Gren broke a smile. "Oh no, we can't have that. If you call someone by name, you'll never know what kind of damage you could do. It could have . . ." she lowered her voice, "'disastrous results'."

"I'm going to tell Hutch in our next session that you were mocking him." Lawson stood up and took a few steps back from Gren.

Gren stood as well. "You wouldn't."

Lawson smiled. "Try and stop me."

He started to run. Gren chased him. They were aware that it was impossible for her to actually catch him without the possibility of suffering some dreadful consequences...whatever those might be.

Chapter Four

Everyone at the Learning Center looked forward to Partnering. Not only was the ceremony itself exciting; the entire rotation was one big party. There were no classes held, no dreams wandered: just games, entertainment, and a lot of special food brought in for the occasion. The older students always enjoyed watching the Whites nervously prepare for their ceremony. Some of them enjoyed it a little bit *too* much.

"You see that little boy over there?" Sham pointed at a young blond boy whose face appeared whiter than his uniform. "Anybody want to make a wager that everything he just ate is about to come back up?"

"Sham, you're terrible!" Calli glanced at him and looked away shyly.

"How long do you give him, and what's the wager?" Titus asked.

"You're terrible, too."

Sham ignored Calli. "I don't know, how about we give him ten hundreds, and the wager is five game tokens?"

Titus watched the boy carefully for a few micros. "Make it four game tokens, and you've got yourself a wager."

"How about I give each of you one of my game tokens and you call it off?" Calli suggested.

"No way!" Sham said. "Make only one token when I could make four?"

"Or lose four," Calli reminded him.

"Look at him, Calli," Sham said. "This is a sure thing."

Tayo winked at Calli. "I'll be right back." She went to the

beverage area, filled a cup, then approached the young White. "I couldn't help but notice that you look a little nervous," she remarked. "Here, drink this. It will settle your stomach." She handed him the cup, being careful to not touch him. Some rules were meant for wandering students of all orbits.

The boy looked at Tayo strangely before drinking the contents. For a micro he looked even more like he was about to be sick. Suddenly he let out a loud burp, smiled, and thanked her. Returning to her own table, Tayo watched as he rejoined the other Whites. "I believe, Sham, that you owe Titus four game tokens."

"The ten hundreds aren't over yet," Sham mumbled, although he reached into his pocket and pulled out the tokens.

Gren loved being outdoors. Most of her sleep tonic–induced nightmares started inside. Her natural dreams were hardly ever scary, and they usually took place in wide-open spaces. Being confined inside for too long always seemed like torture to her. She loved Partnering Rotation; she enjoyed the time off, enjoyed the time outdoors, and...as always...enjoyed her time with Lawson.

Lawson wasn't in the same mood. "They have an odd number this orbit," he remarked after a long silence. "There will have to be one boy/girl partnering."

"So?" Gren was surprised that it seemed to bother Lawson so much. "It can work. We're living proof. How many people from when we were Whites haven't changed partners at least once?"

Lawson shook his head. "But then there are a bunch stupid rules that have to be followed."

Gren didn't want to have that conversation again. "Some of the rules are good. Like having to spend the whole rotation with your partner before the Partnering Ceremony."

Lawson almost broke a smile. "Yeah, they really have to force you and me to spend time together."

"You're right." Gren grinned. "Stupid rules."

"Come on, let's go watch the acting exhibit. It's always funny to see what other people think Dream Wanderers really do."

After the evening feast, everyone gathered in the main auditorium. The Whites sat nervously on the stage, girls on the left side and boys on the right. At the podium in the middle stood Ladinda, the Learning Center's leader. Hutch stood slightly behind her, his dirty blond hair looking lighter than normal in the bright lights. Charla was to his left, and there were more teachers behind them.

Although the first two rows of seats were empty, the Blues sat in the front of the auditorium, followed by the Greens, the Yellows, the Oranges, the Reds, the Purples, and finally the Browns. Each group was slightly smaller than the group behind them, showing that there were no guarantees of making it through an entire orbit. Partners were required to sit together; most of them didn't mind. The ones who did mind wouldn't be partnered for much longer. One female Yellow and one male Purple were each waiting for a new partner their own orbit. They sat with their color but felt very much alone.

Ladinda held up a hand, instantly quieting the auditorium. Everyone knew that obeying Ladinda was one of the most important parts of the program.

"Here we go again!" she said cheerfully. "This is one of my favorite rotations. I hope you've all enjoyed yourselves, a rotation of fun, food, and most importantly . . . no classes!" Everyone laughed. "We have thirty Whites this orbit: fifteen girls and fifteen boys, meaning we'll have a rare girl/boy partnering. For those who think that can't be done, we have two Blues this orbit who have shown us it can!"

Gren felt her face turn red.

"Remember, Whites," Ladinda continued, "this rotation you're starting on a journey. A journey that will be filled with many trials, tests, and tribulations, but a journey that is indeed worth taking. We'll start with the girls. Hutch?"

Hutch stepped forward, not looking all that happy. In his hand was a small bottle.

Ladinda moved a comfortable chair from the side to the center of the stage and Hutch sat down. "For those of you who don't remember, Hutch won't be taking our regular sleep tonic. This is different, it will relax him and help him to dream a bit but he won't be fully asleep."

Hutch drank the bottle's contents, put back his head, and closed his eyes.

"Okay, girls, this is what you're to do," Ladinda instructed. "I need you to try to wander into Hutch's dream. Just a reminder for everyone here; Hutch has orbits of experience and will be able to tell if anyone who is not a female White tries to wander his dream. Dream wandering without permission is against the law, punishable by a heavy fine and time in the labor camp. The sooner you realize that, the better. Now Whites, all you need to do is show up in his dream and say your name, which is the *only* time you'll be allowed to say a name in a dream. Ready, White girls? Try to wander . . . now!"

There were some suppressed laughs from the other colors, especially the Blues, since they were sitting closest. Dream wandering was something that needed to be learned; although the gift came naturally, the skill required orbits of study and practice. The White girls tried their hardest to pop into Hutch's dream by making strange faces or holding their breath. Even Hutch, his eyes closed, was grinning. One girl stood up and raised a hand in front of her, causing a loud burst of laughter from most of the spectators. Even the White boys joined in. She sat down, embarrassed. Everyone watch for several hundreds as the girls squirmed and concentrated.

Finally, Hutch opened his eyes. "Maya and Jilly," was all that he said.

"Maya, Jilly, please step forward," Ladinda commanded. Two girls, both looking excited, came out from the Whites. "You can take your seats in the front row. I want you to spend every micro possible together. Get to know each other." The two girls joined hands and left the stage. "Charla? Your turn."

Charla stepped forward, holding a bottle similar to the one Hutch had already used. "I'm ready," she said, taking a seat in the chair before drinking the tonic.

"Boys, the same rules apply to you," Ladinda instructed. "Just show up in the dream and say your name. Ready?" Most of the boys nodded, some enthusiastically and others with nervous apprehension. "Good. Try to wander . . . now!"

The boys' show was similar to the girls'. Gren couldn't help wondering how some of these children had been accepted into the program, let alone had the slightest chance of completing it. It took even longer for the boys than for the girls. Finally Charla said, "Conner and Nolet," then opened her eyes. Without even being asked, they stepped forward and took their seats.

There were different tests with other teachers to determine the rest of the partners. Some of the tests were intellectual, some were problem-solving, and the rest were just plain luck. At the end of the ceremony there were two Whites left, a boy and a girl.

"Would you two please join me?" Ladinda said. They came to the center of the stage. "What's your name?" she asked the girl.

"Angel," the girl replied quietly. It was the same girl who had stood and embarrassed herself during the wandering test with Hutch.

"Angel, what a pretty name." Ladinda turned toward the boy. "Don't you agree?" She looked at the boy.

"Dod," he said, even softer than Angel had spoken. His face was bright red.

Sham was trying hard to get Calli's attention. Dod was the boy who had looked so nervous at the early morning feast.

"Angel, Dod," Ladinda started, "I want you to know how special it is that you two have been partnered. In fact, if it's not too much trouble, I'd like to ask two Blues, Gren and Lawson, to join us here on stage. They will tell you just how wonderful it can be to be in a boy/girl partnership."

Gren almost leapt out of her seat. Although she didn't particularly like speaking in public (especially without notice), she was more than happy to tell the young Whites how incredible her own partnership was. With Dod's messy blond hair and Angel's long red braids, the new partners reminded Gren of when she and Lawson were partnered. Lawson stood slowly, with much less enthusiasm than Gren.

With a big smile, Gren stood in the center of the stage. "Angel, Dod," she began, "when I was partnered last, my heart sank. But I've come to realize that it was my destiny to be partnered with Lawson. He's amazing. Not only is he fun and easy to work with, but he's also become my best friend. Not having been chosen in the other contests was the only possible way for us to be partnered, and I'm thankful every rotation that we are. It requires more work, especially at first, but with a little extra effort, it is definitely worth it." She smiled again, glanced at Lawson, and moved back from the microphone.

Lawson took Gren's place. "Good luck, kids. You're going to need it." He stepped away, avoiding Gren's stare.

"Well, thank you," Ladinda said, surprised by Lawson's comment. "Please, all four of you, take your seats. That concludes this Partnering Ceremony. Whites, get to know your partners. Your new rooming assignments will be given to you when you arrive back at your dormitories. We'll clear the auditorium in order of color, starting with the Whites."

"Titus, would you please hit Lawson for me?" Gren said as they walked back to their dormitories. She couldn't remember ever being so upset with him. "Although I might be willing to risk getting in trouble by hitting him myself."

Lawson started to explain. "Gren, I was just trying..."

"Oh, shut up!" she interrupted. "Sham, if Titus won't . . ."

"Gladly," Sham replied, and punched Lawson hard in the stomach.

Lawson doubled over in pain. "Okay, I deserved that. But just hear me out. If Ladinda had given us time to prepare something..."

Gren interrupted again. "Then I would have thought of something else to say. Something besides how *wonderful* you are. What a liar I am."

"They *are* going to need luck!" Lawson protested. "Remember how hard it was at first? They kept telling us to 'get to know your partner' and 'spend as much time as possible with your partner,' but we couldn't even be in the same dormitory! All the other partners were roommates...they still are...but we had to become friends over meals and during classes in which we weren't even allowed to talk! And everyone else, when they did something big or important, they were allowed to hug or slap hands or whatever, but we had to fear expulsion if we even stood too close. We *still* do. It's hard, and you know it!"

"Oh, not that again," Gren said. She was painfully aware that her entire group of friends was staring at her. "I'll see you in the morning...maybe." Without looking back she stormed into the girls' dormitory.

Chapter Five

Two rotations after the Partnering, Gren still refused to speak to Lawson. At first she had noticed others whispering behind her back, but the fallout was starting to die down. It didn't matter if others didn't care anymore. She cared, she was angry...and she wanted to make sure Lawson realized it.

Most of all, Gren was dreading their next class with Hutch. She wasn't sure whose dream would be wandered; she hoped it wouldn't be hers. She waited until the last possible micro before trying to slip in the back door.

"I knew I'd find you here!" Lawson said with a little bit of satisfaction as he jumped out in front of her.

"Big surprise...we have a class," Gren replied, trying to move around him. He stood solidly in her way.

"I'm not moving until you talk to me," Lawson said.

"I'm not going to talk to you, so we'll miss class and both get thrown out of the program," Gren shot back. "Just what your parents would have wanted." She immediately regretted the remark. "Lawson, I'm sorry, that was totally uncalled for."

Lawson looked sad. "No, you're right. I would have been a disappointment to my parents."

Gren was exasperated. "I didn't say that. And don't turn this around and make it about my hurting you. You embarrassed me in public. You..."

Lawson moved as close as he could to Gren without touching her. "This has nothing to do with my embarrassing you. I made you feel like our partnering didn't matter. I'm sorry. Being your partner and your friend is the best thing that's ever happened to me."

Gren looked Lawson in the eyes. "Why couldn't you have said that on the stage?"

"Because . . . well . . . they *are* going to need luck. Especially if they stay together as long as we have and start to realize..."

"We're going to be late for class," Gren interrupted. "Upsetting Hutch right now is probably *not* a good idea."

The two partners silently entered the classroom and took their seats. Hutch looked up from the papers in front of him but didn't say a word. The silence soon grew to an uncomfortable level. "So, who gets their dream wandered this time?" Lawson asked at last.

"It's your turn," Gren spit out. She was still upset with Lawson, just not as much as before.

"Neither of you, at least not yet," Hutch answered. "We need to talk."

"About what?" Lawson asked innocently.

"Don't play stupid with me," Hutch instructed. "Let me ask you both flat out: Can you still handle it?"

"Handle what?" Gren asked, although she knew.

"It's not too late to change," Hutch told them. "There's no shame in changing partners. A lot of Blues do in their last orbit. I know that a big deal has been made about your being the first male/female partnering to make it this far; but that just goes to show how difficult it is."

"I don't think it's any more difficult with Lawson than it would be to start over," Gren replied truthfully. "He knows me better than anyone. Calli and Tayo share my room, and I watch them struggle to get to form a partnership that's not even *close* to what I have with Lawson."

"Good answer, Gren," Hutch told her. "You're excused. I'll

see you in two rotations. Lawson, you and I need to talk...man to man."

Gren glanced back at Lawson as she left the room. Suddenly, all of her anger was replaced with fear. They were going to be split up. She knew it.

"Do you know why we have the rules that we have?" Hutch asked Lawson.

"No, sir," he replied quietly.

"Neither do I," Hutch said lightly, "but they're Ladinda's rules, and so we have to follow them. I'm sure she has good reasons." He unlocked the cabinet and took out a bottle of tonic. "Let's try an experiment. This isn't the same sleep tonic we usually use. This one won't induce nightmares. In fact, this is the tonic that licensed Dream Wanderers use about half of the time. You'll learn all about it when you're an apprentice. Hop on the table. I'm going to wander your dream."

Lawson nervously approached the dream table. He didn't like what was happening at all. "Do I have to?"

"I won't hurt you, I promise. And yes, you have to. Unless you'd rather be have Ladinda wander."

Lawson sat on the table and drank the contents of the bottle.

Hutch sat down next to the table. "Not bad, huh? It's a lot better than the swill you usually have to drink. Okay, Lawson, you know what to do. Close your eyes and relax."

Lawson lay down and closed his eyes. He felt different than normal. He didn't realize he was dreaming, even when he heard Hutch's voice.

"Walk forward," Hutch ordered. His voice was calm yet filled with authority. "Keep going. You're almost at the lake. You know how much you like the lake. It's the most beautiful spot on campus."

Lawson did as he was told. Soon the lake was in view.

"Look, up ahead. It's Gren! You really need to talk to her, tell her you're sorry for embarrassing her."

"I don't see her," Lawson said.

"She's over there, behind that tree," Hutch continued. "The one Titus is standing in front of. Calli and Tayo are there, too. I wonder why they're standing in a line like that. It's almost like they're guarding something."

Lawson's friends stood in front of him, blocking the tree. "Let me by," he said. "I need to talk to Gren."

"Sorry, can't do that," Titus replied in a voice that sounded a lot like Hutch. "Sham asked me to keep everyone away."

"Sham? What does Sham have to do with anything? He's not even here. And where's Gren? I really need to apologize to her."

"Go away," Titus/Hutch said loudly.

"No!"

"Go around to the other side," Hutch, back in wandering mode, recommended. "Fake them out. Then you'll be able to see Gren."

Lawson pretended he was going to leave, but ran around Calli and made it behind the tree. There he saw Gren. He stopped and stared for a few micros. Gren was with Sham. They were kissing. "No!" Lawson screamed.

Sham let go of Gren. "Why not?" he asked, his voice sounding a lot like Hutch.

"It's against the rules," Lawson reminded him, not sure what else to say.

Sham/Hutch laughed. "Haven't you heard? Ladinda changed the rules. That 'no physical contact with students of the opposite gender' rule? It's gone! So Gren and I are planning on doing *a lot* of touching..."

"You can't," Lawson said. "Not with Gren."

"Why not with Gren? She's pretty, funny, smart, and a lot of fun to be with. I'm surprised you didn't think of it yourself." Sham turned back toward Gren. "Now where were we?"

"No!" Lawson screamed again.

"Why not?" Sham/Hutch asked for a third time. "You still haven't given me a good enough reason."

"Because I'm in love with her!" Lawson yelled at the top of his lungs. "Okay? I'm in love with Gren!"

Hutch sighed as he gently shook Lawson. "Sit up slowly, son. This tonic takes a little bit longer to wear off."

Lawson looked at Hutch. "That was cruel."

"*That,*" Hutch said, "is the power of a licensed Dream Wanderer. I needed information and I manipulated your dream until I found it. I'm sorry I had to do that to you. And I'm sorry for my recommendation."

A unit later, Gren and Lawson sat in Ladinda's office. Hutch stood behind them. Ladinda sat at her desk. Gren tried not to cry; she knew it would only hurt her case. Lawson stared at his feet.

"I think," Ladinda said cheerfully, "it's partly my fault. I was so happy we had a boy/girl partnering make it all the way to Blue that I didn't pay attention to the dynamics of your relationship. I truly regret that. I believed it was working."

"It *is* working," Gren said boldly. She knew better than to question Ladinda's wisdom, but she couldn't believe that Lawson might no longer be her partner.

Ladinda smiled. "You're proving my point, my dear. The problem is that there are no open Blue partners right now. You both show so much potential; I want you to continue practicing. So this is what we're going to do. You can remain partners, *for now*, until something else opens up. But there will be a special set of rules for you both to follow. You can walk to and from classes together *as long as someone else is present*. You can sit at the same table at mealtime *but not next to each other*. And you can be together for any event that requires you to be with your partner. But that's it. I don't want you to be alone with each other...ever. No more walks, no more sitting under the trees, no more time at the lake if the other one is there, even with a group. Do I make myself clear?"

"Yes, ma'am," they said in unison.

"Lawson," Ladinda continued, "you'll need to find another place to spend breaks for the rest of this orbit."

Lawson opened his mouth to protest. "But..."

"It's better than being thrown out of the program." Ladinda leaned forward. "We'll be keeping an eye on both of you. If I see *any* violations of the rules, you'll both be expelled. That includes almost touching and pretending it's an accident, as I've noticed you have a tendency to do. Understood?"

"Yes, ma'am," they replied again.

Ladinda stood up. "Good. Lawson, you may escort Gren back to the female dormitory, so the two of you will have one last time to discuss how unfair my rules are. You're both dismissed."

Chapter Six

Three lunar cycles later, Gren and Lawson were still partnered. The special rules, created just for them, continued. Neither Gren nor Lawson was enjoying their final orbit as much as they had hoped. School break was coming up, a period of one lunar cycle away from the Learning Center. Gren dreaded it; it was the first time she could remember that she wouldn't be with Lawson.

"Come on, Gren, cheer up," Tayo told her friend. "It won't be all that bad. You'll have the chance to spend some quality time with your parents and your little sister, just the four of you. That's something you haven't done in orbits."

"My parents really *like* Lawson," Gren said. "They're acting like this is all my fault. I don't know what I could have done differently."

"I feel sorry for Lawson," Calli added, trying to lighten the mood. "He's stuck spending his entire break with Sham."

"Then I feel sorry for Sham," Gren replied. She was almost at her class.

The one good thing that had happened since the new rules went into effect was that, for the time being, Gren and Lawson no longer had to have their dreams wandered. Instead, they practiced wandering the younger colors' dreams. Ladinda had decided that, since they seemed to have a lot in common with Angel and Dod, the Blues would work closely with them. It gave the younger students a chance to see how dreams were wandered; it gave Gren and Lawson a different type of practice.

Lawson, with Angel and Dod close behind him, approached

Gren and her friends. "Will you meet us here after class?" he asked Calli and Tayo. "I wouldn't want to get in trouble for talking to my partner." His voice was heavy with sarcasm.

"Sure," Calli said. She knew there had been several tests to make sure Gren and Lawson followed the rules. Fortunately, they had passed them all, but Lawson was becoming more and more bitter. "If we're not here before you're done, well, be careful."

Lawson rolled his eyes. "As always."

Together, with Angel and Dod between them, Lawson and Gren entered the building. "How have you been?" Lawson asked over the top of the Whites' heads. "We haven't had the chance to talk for so long. Any special plans for the break?" He hated being reduced to making small talk with his best friend.

"Nothing special. Just spending time with my family," Gren replied. "It's going to be strange without you there. I received a message from them a little while ago. Winnie's really disappointed."

"It will do you and your little sister a lot of good to spend some time, just the two of you, for a change," Lawson said without much conviction. "We were partnered before she was born; she's never had you to herself."

"She just got her placement test back," Gren told him. "She's being recommended for Culinary Arts."

"Good!" Lawson said. "Anything but Dream Wanderer."

"What are you two talking about?" Dod asked. He was getting used to them talking over the top of his head.

"Nothing," Lawson answered. "Let's get to class."

As they entered the classroom, Hutch was nowhere to be seen. Gren and Lawson assumed his absence was another test and went to opposite sides on the room. Angel joined Gren, while Dod followed Lawson.

"Can I talk to you about something?" Dod asked.

"Sure, kid," Lawson replied. He knew the boy looked up to him, but he couldn't comprehend why. "What's up?"

"It's Angel," Dod whispered.

"What about her?" Lawson glanced over at Gren, who was having a quiet conversation with Angel.

"She's a . . . girl."

"And?"

"I don't understand girls," Dod admitted quietly.

Lawson grinned. "See, kid, there's your problem. Don't think of Angel as a girl...that will only get you in trouble around here. Think of her as . . . well . . . as one of the guys. She can be a really good friend if you both make a little bit of effort. Just don't think of her as a girl, ever."

In the far corner of the room, Gren and Angel spoke softly. "Can I talk to you about something?" Angel asked.

"Of course," Gren replied. She really liked the girl, who reminded Gren of her sister.

"It's about Dod," Angel started. "He's a boy, and . . ."

Gren glanced over at Lawson and smiled. "Being partnered with a boy can be a wonderful thing, no matter how big a jerk he is at the Partnering Ceremony."

"Then why do you two have special rules?"

"I thought this was about you and Dod!" Gren thought for a couple of micros. "Lawson and I have special rules because some people thought we were becoming *too* close. But I don't understand. How can you be too close to your best friend or your partner?"

At that micro, Hutch walked in. "Gren," he said sternly, making it obvious that he had heard part of their conversation.

"Sorry, sir," Gren replied, not really sure what she had done wrong.

"Let's get right to it," Hutch said. "Dod, your dream will be wandered. One person will do the actual wandering. The other two, along with me, will observe. Angel, you've made remarkable progress in the short time you've been here. I have no doubt you'll be able to keep up. Since this is our last class before the break, Dod, I'll let you pick. Who do you want to guide you, Lawson or Gren?"

"Lawson," Dod said quickly.

"Good, Lawson needs the practice more than Gren does," Hutch said. "Hop up on the table. Quickly...we don't have all rotation."

Dod tried to look around the large, dark cave. A small amount of light shone from a hole in the ceiling, but it didn't provide any comfort. "I can't see," he said loudly.

"Reach to your right," Lawson's voice told him. "There's a torch. Use it and you'll be able to see."

"I'm not allowed to play with fire," Dod said.

"No, it's a magic torch," Lawson added quickly. "Just wave your hand over the top and it will provide a strong, *safe* beam of light." Dod did as he was told, and the torch soon provided a steady glow. "Search the walls, you'll find your way out."

Dod used the torch to locate the cave wall. He saw a small pathway through the rocks. "Should I take it?"

"Yes," Lawson's comforting voice told him. "Just follow where it goes. You'll be out in no time."

As he continued to walk, Dod could hear water dripping slowly from somewhere in the cave. It echoed eerily. He continued to walk, torch held in front of him, through the narrow space between the rocks. The rock walls grew closer and closer together, until he was scared to go on. "I can't make it! I'll get stuck."

"You won't get stuck." Lawson's voice was soothing, but also slightly in command. "Just push through and you'll be in a larger cave. The exit will then be straight ahead. You can do it."

"If you say so." Dod held his breath and squeezed through the narrow passageway. He made it, only to discover that the promised larger cave wasn't empty. It was filled with girls with long, red braids and wearing White uniforms. "No!" Dod screamed. Angel's slight laugh was heard, a reminder that the dream was being observed as well as wandered.

"It's okay," Lawson told him. "There are a lot worse things in life than a bunch of girls."

"Like what?" Dod asked. It was unusual to be holding a regular conversation during a session, but it was possible.

"Like being told you can't be with them," Lawson replied with anger. "Like spending orbits with someone until you get so close that you know each other's thoughts...then having it all taken away from you because someone is scared you might actually care about your partner." Lawson's voice continued to fill with rage. "Like stupid rules that can expel you for touching someone's hand!"

"That's enough," Hutch's voice said. He switched to wandering mode. "You can walk through them; none of those girls will bother you. The mouth of the cave is visible from where you are. Just walk to it, and you'll be out." Dod did as he was told, and soon the light of the rotation shone on his face. He breathed an audible sigh of relief, happy to be out of there.

"Dod, are you okay?" Hutch shook him gently. The dream was over, but the young boy didn't seem to want to wake up.

Dod waited a few micros, then yawned. "Yeah, I'm okay."

He sat up and grinned. "That was fun. Can I have Lawson wander my dreams all the time?"

"No," Hutch said sternly. "You and Angel are excused." Both stayed where they were. "Now!"

"Come on, Dod," Angel said, "I think we have to leave."

"You'd better not mention anything about my dream," Dod told his partner.

"I won't, I promise. It's against the rules to make fun of someone's dream." The two Whites walked out the door.

"Close it behind you," Hutch called. He waited until the door slammed shut, then he looked directly at Lawson. "What was that?" He shook his head. "And the session started out with so much promise!"

Lawson didn't say a word.

"Dod seemed to like it," Gren pointed out in his defense.

Hutch shook his head again. "That doesn't matter. If this had been a *real* session..."

"But it wasn't," Lawson interrupted. "Nothing about it was real. It was a nightmare induced by some stupid tonic. The only things that are real in this whole stupid place are my feelings for Gren, and you're trying to take those away from me!" He stood up and headed for the door.

"Lawson, if you leave now," Hutch began, "I'll have to..."

"*I don't care anymore!*" Lawson screamed. He ran out the door.

"He's on edge," Gren tried to explain. "It's hard for him, with his parents being dead. He's come to think of my family as his family as well, and with Ladinda not allowing him to spend break with us . . ."

"That's no excuse," Hutch said. "Gren, if you go after him, you'll both be expelled."

"I understand." Gren stayed where she was, not knowing what else to do.

Chapter Seven

It bothered Gren a little that she didn't see Lawson at the evening meal, but she'd expected it. He needed time to cool off. Not seeing him the next morning bothered her a lot more. She arrived for the morning meal early and waited anxiously for Titus and Sham to show up. They were Lawson's roommates; they would assure her that everything was fine.

"Hey, Gren, where's Lawson?" Sham asked as he took his seat.

"You haven't seen him?" she asked, worried.

"No, he didn't come home last night," Titus replied.

"We thought for sure you'd know where he was," Sham said. "He never does anything without telling you about it."

"I'm going to look for him," Gren informed her friends.

"You can't do that. You'll be expelled." Calli had just sat down next to her.

"I don't care anymore," Gren said. She picked up some bread from her plate, wrapped it carefully in a napkin, and stuck it in her pocket. Seeing everyone staring at her she explained, "When I find Lawson, he's going to be hungry."

"I'll help you look," Tayo said. "We all will. But we shouldn't all go at once. It would be too obvious."

"Since there are no classes, we can meet at the lake, every two units," Calli suggested. "That way we'll all know what's going on, fill each other in."

"Thanks," Gren said. "I'll see you in two units."

After finishing their meal, Calli and Tayo started to search

together. Every time they saw a glimpse of blue, they thought it was Lawson, but they didn't find him. Two units later, they met Sham and Titus by the lake. Gren was nowhere to be seen.

"She must have found him," Titus commented. "The two of them took off together."

"She wouldn't have done that," Calli said. "She knows we're all worried."

"Oh, come on," Titus argued. "It's not like there isn't a certain rule that the two of them would like to break. That's why they've almost been split up. All Lawson ever does is mumble Gren's name in his sleep. It makes it pretty hard to not wander his dreams sometimes."

"Gren gets embarrassed talking about Lawson and the future," Tayo noted.

"No!" Calli raised her voice. "They *didn't* run away. Something doesn't feel right. I don't know what it is, but something is terribly out of place."

"Everyone has to go to the auditorium." Lanna startled the group. She and Macy had approached from behind.

"But the farewell speech isn't until tonight," Sham said.

"All I know is that Hutch just told us everyone is to meet in the auditorium immediately," Lanna said.

"We'd better get going," Macy said. The group took a few steps.

"Wait a hundred. What's that?" Calli pointed toward a small portion of blue fabric, floating in the water. Sham pulled it out. There was also a piece of torn material with a strange symbol on it. He was the only one who noticed the second piece of cloth.

"I wonder if that's from Lawson's uniform," Tayo said.

"I doubt it." Sham glanced at the strange design, then put the wet bits of cloth in his pocket.

A unit later, the auditorium was filled with students, sitting with their colors. Ladinda was on the stage, counting heads. When she was satisfied that everyone was there, she raised her arm and quieted the crowd. "I know that this is highly unusual," she said, "but we have a very serious matter at hand. Most of you here know Lawson and Gren, partnered Blues." Their pictures, blown up large for everyone to see, appeared behind Ladinda. "If you see either one of them, you must report it to a teacher or to me immediately. If you see them during the break, contact the authorities. The only way we can help them is if we can talk to them."

There was a murmuring throughout the room. Finally Angel raised her hand. "I saw Gren this morning."

"We know Gren was at the morning meal," Ladinda replied. "We think she found Lawson not long after that. In case you don't realize how severe this is, a serious crime has been committed. Several cases of sleep tonic have been stolen. Quite a few people have told me Lawson jokes constantly about becoming a Dream Wanderer on the Black Market. We need to stop him before he actually does. Right now, the consequences aren't dire, but if he goes through with his plans..." She let her sentence drop. "Lawson is one of us, as is Gren. She would be an accessory. So keep your eyes open, and report anything you might find out."

Ladinda smiled. "Enjoy your break, one and all. One last thing. I need to see Gren's and Lawson's roommates in my office in ten hundreds. Everyone else is excused."

Ladinda's office usually seemed spacious, but with Lawson's two roommates and Gren's four, it was cramped. Ladinda was once again sitting at her desk. The girls were seated; the two boys stood behind them. Ladinda looked sternly at the teenagers scattered before her. "I want information, and I want it now. What was said this morning?"

The group looked at each other. "I wasn't there," Lanna said quickly. "Neither was Macy. When we got up this morning, Gren had already left."

Ladinda looked at Lanna. "Did she saying anything to you last night?"

"No, ma'am," Lanna replied. "Macy and I were getting in some extra practice, like Hutch suggested. When we got in, Gren was already in bed, although I don't think she was sleeping. We didn't hear about Lawson until this morning."

"You are both dismissed," Ladinda told them, "but if you think of anything, let me know." Lanna and Macy left the room. "You two," Ladinda said to Sham and Titus, "sit." They took the vacant seats. Ladinda stared at each person seated before her. "What was said this morning?"

Calli glanced at her partner. "Gren said she was going to look for Lawson. We said we'd help. That's all."

"Did you find anything?"

"No," Sham said quickly.

Ladinda leaned forward. Her normally pleasant face looked cold. "Nothing? Nothing at all?"

Sham reached into his pocket, careful to pull out only the blue cloth. "Just a bit of fabric. It could have come from any Blue's uniform."

"Where was it?" Ladinda asked.

"In the lake," Sham said. "At the water's edge."

Ladinda remained silent for several micros as she examined the torn blue cloth. "If you think of anything else, let me know. You're excused." Everyone stood. "Just remember: You won't help your friends by keeping things from me. I'm the only one who can save their careers...and possibly their lives."

As Sham packed for the break, he debated telling Titus about the other piece of material he'd found. He decided against it. If people could show up in others dreams, couldn't other people somehow eavesdrop on conversations?

"Let's get together in a couple of rotations," Sham suggested, breaking the silence. "Calli and Tayo, too. We don't too far apart, and I think a little bit of fun would do us all some good."

"You're probably right," Titus agreed. "Maybe by then one of us will have heard from Lawson or Gren."

"I doubt it," Sham said as he knew something.

"Why?"

Sham shook his head. "I don't know. No reason, just a feeling.

Why don't we meet at my place in three rotations? Calli and Tayo, too."

"Won't your parents mind?" Titus asked.

Sham smiled. "Not at all." He failed to remind his friend that his parents would be on vacation in two rotations.

Chapter Eight

"Gren, wake up." Gren recognized Lawson's voice but wasn't sure if he was actually there, or if he had broken the law by wandering into her dream. She opened her eyes, unable to see much because of the dim light.

"Lawson?" Gren squinted, trying to figure out where she was. She was sure that she was in the classroom, having a dream wandered by Lawson with Hutch observing. The strange thing was that it didn't feel like a dream. Her eyes adjusted. The room was small, dirty, and musty. At the front, there was a door with bars on it. She didn't see her partner anywhere. "Lawson, where are you?"

"Over here." There was a hole in the wall, which someone reached through. "See my hand?" There were several smaller holes; the wall didn't seem very well built.

"Where are we?" Gren asked.

"I have no idea," Lawson replied, "but we're obviously not at the Learning Center anymore."

"Is this another test?" Gren asked.

Lawson sighed. "No, I think we're in bigger trouble than that."

"How did we get here?" Gren wanted to know.

"I'm not sure," Lawson replied. "Everything is kind of blurry in my mind. I remember I stormed out of Hutch's class and went for a walk to calm down. I sat down for a little while. The next thing I remember, I woke up here. They brought you in a couple of units ago, and I've been trying to get you to wake up ever since. What do you remember?"

"I went searching for you, after the morning meal," Gren said, trying to concentrate. "I was supposed to meet Calli and everybody by the lake two units later. I thought you might be there, so that's where I started looking. Someone grabbed me from behind. I fought," she looked down at her sleeve, realizing that it had been torn, "but there were two of them. They put something over my face. That's all I remember."

"I wonder what they want with us," Lawson said.

"Not wonder, wander!" A short, heavy man stood outside the door. He laughed, pleased at his own joke.

"What does that mean?" Lawson asked, his voice trembling. He couldn't see the man, just hear his voice.

"Ya'll find out soon enough," the man replied. He smiled, revealing that he was missing several teeth. "They call me Handy. You two kids aren't goin' to give me any trouble, are ya?" Handy fumbled with some keys, then opened Gren's door.

Gren backed away. "No, sir."

Handy laughed again. "Ya don't have to call me sir, little girl. Just do what I say, and don't give me any trouble. Because if ya do, see this?" He held up something that looked liked a thin, shiny stick. "Hey, boy, stay away from the wall a micro, will ya?" Handy touched something on the end of stick, and suddenly a large chunk of the wall was missing. Dust flew everywhere. Both Gren and Lawson started to cough, but it didn't seem to faze Handy. "Come on, boy, ya can make it through there, can't ya? No sense in havin' to find the key again."

Lawson crawled through the hole. He reached for Gren, but she backed away out of habit. Some rules were hard to forget. "Are you okay?" he asked her.

Gren nodded.

"Of course she's okay," Handy said. "It was just a little sleepin' potion that ya both got. Nothing like that sleep tonic ya Dream Wanderers use, but it'll work to knock ya out for a while."

It occurred to Gren that Handy had mentioned wandering twice. "We're not Dream Wanderers. We're just students."

Handy smiled, showing the gaps in his teeth again. His clothes were dirty, and there was an unfamiliar symbol on one sleeve. The bottom of the other sleeve was missing. "Ya might be just students, but ya're two of the best students in the whole Learnin' Center. We've been watching ya for a long time now. We also know that ya'll do anythin' for each other. And we know that Learnin' Center of yours has a bunch of really dumb rules that neither of ya like to follow. Now, come with me. Captain Fia would like to meet both of ya." He pushed the stick into Gren's back. "Just a warning. I don't want to hurt either of ya, but one wrong move, and your girlfriend here gets it."

"I'm not his girlfriend," Gren said out automatically.

Handy led Gren and Lawson through several rooms and hallways. Gren was growing tired. Her first thought was that it was an effect of the sleeping potion, but why would that make her legs feel heavy?

At the top of a ramp they entered some kind of control area. There were several people present, but the only one who took notice of them was a tall, slender woman with short, straight, black hair. She was wearing a dark gray uniform with an insignia on her collar. A strange symbol marked both sleeves, the same symbol Handy wore. Glancing around, Gren noticed that everyone seemed to wear the symbol.

"Gren, Lawson," the woman said. "How nice of you to join us. I'm Captain Fia."

"How do you know our names?" Lawson asked.

Captain Fia smiled. "We've been watching you for a long time. Partnered Blues, a male/female partnering that made it *almost* all the way through the program. I'm impressed."

"What do you know about the program?" Gren asked.

Captain Fia continued to smile. "Quite a bit, my friend. I once attended the Learning Center, myself. I, too, was partnered with someone from the 'other' gender. We made it to Green, but we were growing up, and there were so many rules to follow. . . Maybe you know him. His name is Hutch."

"You were partnered with Hutch?" Lawson asked quickly.

It dawned on Gren that, if Captain Fia had been watching them, she would know without a doubt that they knew Hutch. It was obviously a trick to make them trust her.

"Yes," Fia continued, "we were partnered as Browns. We used to take long walks by the lake, talking about the future. But then I was blamed for something I didn't even do. A word of advice: follow all their rules. If you're expelled and they remove the gift of Dream Wandering, it hurts!"

"What does this have to do with us?" Gren asked.

Captain Fia put an arm around Gren's shoulder. "Come with me. There's something I want to show you." She led them to a large window. All that it revealed were stars and darkness. "You've probably guessed we're *not* at the Learning Center. To be honest, we're not even on Terra. We're on our way to Abacu."

"Abacu?" Gren repeated.

"That's not possible," Lawson added.

"Oh, but it is, my dear Lawson," Fia said. "That's the problem with Terrans, they're so narrow minded. They can't see past their own back yard. But there's a big, exciting universe out there...and you're going to have the opportunity to see some of it. You'll have to make some minor adjustments...for example, gravity is slightly stronger on Abacu, which this ship reflects, but you're in for the adventure of a lifetime. Something that you'll be bragging to Sham and Calli about for orbits."

"What if we don't want to go?" Gren ignored the mention of their friends.

Captain Fia disregarded the question. "Handy, take our young guests back to their accommodations. Let's give them some time to get used to their new situation."

"Whatever ya say, Captain." Handy pulled out the sticklike weapon and pointed it at Gren. "Come on, kids."

Neither Lawson nor Gren said a word until they were back in Gren's cell and the door had been locked. Gren sat on the floor and put her head down. She started to cry.

Lawson approached her. "Gren, it's okay," he said soothingly. "We'll figure something out." He reached for her, but Gren moved away.

"No," she sobbed. "We still can't break the rules."

Lawson sat next to her, close, but not touching. "We've got bigger problems than the Learning Center's stupid rules."

"Think about it," Gren said, wiping her eyes. She kept her voice down, in case someone was listening. "Captain Fia knows all about the Learning Center. She obviously has an agenda. If we break one rule that we've lived with all these orbits, she's going to think we'll be willing to break more."

Lawson sighed. "You're right. I wonder what she's up to."

Gren lowered her voice even further. "My guess is she's going to try to make us trust her. So we have to make sure we don't. We can pretend we do after a little while."

"That's not a bad idea," Lawson whispered. "What about Handy?"

"He's probably going to play the bad guy," Gren guessed. "They'll make us afraid of him so we'll run to Fia."

"What do you think it's all about?"

"It must have something to do with wandering. That's the only thing that makes sense. We both know wandering can be used for good or bad. Hutch has drilled that into our heads for orbits."

Lawson almost chuckled. "Hutch. Do you think Fia really was his partner?"

Gren shook her head. "She's the right age, but Hutch knew we were struggling. Hutch knew *you* were struggling. If he understood from experience, I think he would have said something."

"You're probably right," Lawson said. "I wonder if we'll ever see him...or anyone else...again." There was a loud rumbling sound. "Sorry. I haven't eaten in what feels like orbits."

"I forgot," Gren replied. She reached into her pocket and pulled out the badly flattened bread. "I figured you'd be hungry."

"You want some?"

"No. I don't think I could eat if I tried." As Lawson ate, Gren again put her head down. The tears started to flow once more, but she cried quietly. She didn't want Lawson to know.

Chapter Nine

Three rotations later, Calli and Tayo flew Calli's glidemobile to Sham's dwelling. Titus had arrived a couple of units earlier. They sat around a table.

"My parents almost didn't leave," Sham told his friends. "I talked them into it. They've had reservations for this vacation for almost two orbits. I told them I didn't want them to end up on the waiting list again. But once the System Workers showed up, they were really worried."

"I know what you mean," Tayo said. "They searched our dwelling, too. My mother is pretty freaked out. She's never met Gren or Lawson, but she's acting like they're criminals."

"My parents wanted me to stay home," Calli added. "They never would have let me come here, so I had to tell them that I'm staying with Tayo for a few rotations. I said Ladinda recommended it, so we don't end up having to change partners again."

"I just want to know what happened to Lawson and Gren," Titus said. "I'd still think maybe Gren found Lawson and they ran off together...except for the missing sleep tonic. I don't care what anyone says; I don't for a micro believe Lawson stole it."

"I think there's something bigger going on than a couple of students running away," Sham said slowly. "Remember when we found that piece of torn Blue uniform by the lake?" Everyone nodded. "Well, I didn't tell Ladinda, but I also found this." He showed them the other ripped cloth.

Calli picked it up and looked closely. "It looks like part of a sleeve."

"It wasn't there before the morning meal," Sham said. "I went down there, looking for Lawson." He took the sleeve back from Calli. "See this, here?" Everyone nodded again. "That's a symbol of some type. I've seen it in one place before."

"Where?" Tayo asked.

"There's a man who lives not far from here," Sham explained. "I used to visit him all the time when I was younger, but my parents decided he was a bad influence. I don't know, I guess they thought he'd get me kicked out of the program."

"Why?" Calli wanted to know.

"Well," Sham started, "Roy is a little bit . . . odd. He thinks he's from Abacu."

"Wait a micro," Titus said. "You're talking about *him*? From what you've told Lawson and me, Roy is more than a little bit odd, he's outright crazy!"

Sham shrugged his shoulders. "Yeah, that too. But if my hunch is right, Roy will be able to help us."

Less than a unit later, the four of them were crammed into Calli's glidemobile. They stopped in front of a dwelling that Calli hoped was the wrong place. Weeds sprouted everywhere; it looked like no one had lived there in orbits. Instead of shiny silver like most Terran dwellings, the main building was a dull gray. A smaller shack behind looked like one good gust of wind would topple it over. Sham immediately jumped out of the vehicle and headed up the overgrown front path.

"You have *got* to be kidding," Tayo exclaimed. "Are you sure somebody lives here?"

As if to answer her question, the front door slid slightly open. "Who is it? I'm armed!" To prove it, something sprayed out the door.

Everyone took cover, but then Titus reached out his hand.

"It's water."

"Roy?" Sham called. "I don't know if you remember me. It's Sham. I used to stop by all the time when I was younger, until..."

"Until ya entered that *Dream Wanderin'* program," Roy called back in a mocking voice. "Ya got too good to visit. Ya thought I was crazy, just like the rest of them."

"No! I never thought that. I always loved coming here. My father made me stop."

"What do ya want with me now?" Roy yelled.

"I need your help," Sham paused. "*We* need your help. I've brought some friends from school. Some other friends of ours have disappeared, and..."

"I don't know nothin' about it!" Roy shouted. "I wasn't good enough for ya for the last few orbits. Leave me alone now!"

"It's concerning Abacu," Sham yelled back. "And this." He placed a rock in the sleeve, rolled the whole thing up into a ball, and threw it at the door.

The door opened a bit more and a hand retrieved the cloth.

After several micros the door opened the rest of the way, revealing Roy. "Well why didn't ya say so? Come on in, all of ya."

The inside of Roy's dwelling was different from what any of them had expected. It was spotless. Everyone sat down, and Roy gave each of them a beverage. "Ya've certainly gotten big. I never would have recognized ya."

"It's been a while," Sham replied, slightly embarrassed. Being in Roy's dwelling brought back a flood of memories. He had loved stopping by when he was younger, but once he was accepted into the Dream Wandering program, his parents put an end to the visits. Dream Wanderers were respectable, and Sham's parents thought Roy was anything but. "I'm sorry. I wanted to keep coming, but . . . I don't know . . ."

"Forget it, ya're here now," Roy said with a grin. "Who are your friends?"

"This is Titus, my partner in the program. And these are Calli and Tayo."

"Nice to meet ya," Roy replied, "but I was talkin' about your friends that ya said were in trouble. The friends who disappeared."

"Oh," Sham said. "Their names are Lawson and Gren. They're also Blues in the program, the longest male/female partnering ever. But Lawson was having a problem with some of the rules..."

"Ya mean hormones," Roy corrected.

"Probably," Sham agreed. "He stormed out of a session, and no one has seen him since. Gren went looking for him the next morning, and then she disappeared, as well. Some people say they ran off together."

"But ya don't believe that. Why not?"

"There was some sleep tonic stolen," Sham responded. "Several cases. Lawson may like to skirt around the edge of the rules sometimes, but he's not a thief."

"Sleep tonic. Powerful stuff in the wrong hands. Tell me about this." Roy held up the sleeve. "Where did ya find it?"

"In the water, at the lake at the Learning Center," Sham informed him. "There was also a piece of a Blue uniform there, but I had to turn that in to Ladinda."

"It was probably from Gren's uniform," Roy commented. "I bet she put up a fight! I'm glad ya didn't turn this in, no one from the Learnin' Center would have been able to help ya."

"Do you know what it is?" Calli asked.

"Of course," Roy boasted. "It's the symbol of the Royal

Abacuan Army."

Tayo looked skeptical. "How would you know?"

Roy smiled. He stood and walked over to a chest in the corner. He pulled something out and turned around. "Does this answer your question?" He was holding a full uniform with the symbol on both sleeves. "I used to be a member."

Chapter Ten

Gren was scared. Neither she nor Lawson had seen anyone since Handy had returned them to the cells. Gren couldn't shake the feeling that, although they seemed to be alone, they were being watched.

Lawson hadn't returned to his original cell. Instead, he had fallen asleep on the floor near Gren's cot. He appeared to be dreaming. She knew she shouldn't, but Gren decided to wander. Since they both suspected they were being watched, it might be the only chance they would have to communicate privately. She closed her eyes and pretended to be falling asleep, as well. She would have to be quiet, and she would have to wander farther into a dream than she had ever been allowed to go before. She hoped that whoever was watching them wouldn't know what she was doing. She doubted she was up to the challenge.

At first, Gren felt like she was in totally unfamiliar surroundings. She had been wandering Lawson's dreams for orbits, but the sleep tonic they usually used for practice induced nightmares. This was just an ordinary dream. She could see Lawson up ahead, sitting with someone near the lake. It took Gren a micro to realize that *she* was the person he was sitting with. It felt strange, looking at herself through Lawson's dream. She listened to the two of them, while trying to figure out how to approach her partner.

Lawson moved his hand closer to the dream-Gren, and she laughed quietly. "Okay, watch out," he said. "This time I'm really going to do it." He placed his hand on hers and then pulled it away abruptly. "Oh, no! The planet has stopped spinning! We're going to fall off!"

Dream-Gren laughed again. "Lawson, we're too good for this program and its stupid rules. Let's run away. We don't need anything but you and me and our..."

The real Gren cleared her throat, not wanting to hear the rest of the sentence. "Enough nonsense, Lawson," she said. She knew she wasn't supposed to call him by name while wandering, but for some reason she thought that, in their current situation, it was a good idea. "We need to talk."

Lawson looked at the Gren sitting next to him before looking around, confused. "What's going on?"

"I'm wandering your dream," Gren replied. She knew he could hear her, but it wasn't possible to see a wanderer. She felt bad for confusing him. She realized she'd broken several rules of wandering already, but she didn't care.

"It's against the law to wander someone's dream without permission," Lawson reminded her.

"It's also against the law to kidnap two people and drag them off to another planet," Gren said.

"Oh, yeah. I forgot about that." The lake and dream-Gren disappeared, and the surroundings changed into the cell. Lawson was still asleep. If he had awakened, the wandering would have ended.

"This might be the only way that you and I can talk in private," Gren said, "so let's agree right now that we can wander each other's dreams."

"Okay, as long as you don't hold anything you see against me," Lawson teased.

Gren ignored the comment. She reminded herself that he was sleeping and probably didn't realize that she was actually in his dream. She wondered briefly if he had ever dreamed that he was being wandered. She certainly had. "You need to concentrate," Gren said at last. "You need to stay asleep so we can communicate, but be constantly aware that this is really happening."

"Sure, no problem," Lawson replied. "Whatever you say."

"So, what are we going to do?" Gren asked, allowing some of her fear to creep into her voice.

"Simple. I'll jump that Handy guy, you'll grab that stick thingy, and we'll blast our way out of here."

"How do we get past Captain Fia? Or off the ship, for that matter?"

"Simple," Lawson repeated. "It will be just like that other dream. You know, the one I have about you almost every night, the one where we run away from the Learning Center. There are just a few more people in it this time."

"Lawson," Gren said, growing slightly impatient, "this is real. We've been taken away from the Learning Center against our wills, and I'm trying to talk to you now by wandering your dream."

"You *always* say that it's real, Gren. Every time. Then I wake up, and it was just a dream. So don't try to tell me that this isn't a dream now."

"It *is* a dream now," Gren said. "A dream that I'm wandering because we need to talk."

Lawson smiled for a micro. "That would explain why I can't see you. What a nice little twist for this dream! But I know it isn't real, because the real Gren would *never* wander someone's dream without permission."

"Lawson, you just gave me permission! *This is real!*"

"Okay, Gren, I'll play along," Lawson said. "This time,

we've been kidnapped by some woman, and we're being taken to some planet."

"Captain Fia said Abacu," Gren reminded him.

"Yeah, right, Abacu. So what are we going to do?"

Gren sighed. "That's why I decided to wander your dream. So we could figure out what we should do."

"I have an idea!" Lawson said enthusiastically.

For the first time in units Gren felt a little bit of hope. "What?"

"Let's go back to sleep," Lawson suggested. "Then maybe an idea will come to us in our dreams."

"You *are* asleep," Gren said.

"I am?" Lawson sounded surprised. "That's good. I'd hate to think we've *really* been kidnapped."

Gren sighed a second time before removing herself from Lawson's dream. She felt worse, not better, and more scared than she had realized. She closed her eyes, the emotional exhaustion even more powerful than the physical, and somehow, drifted off to sleep herself.

A unit later, Lawson lay on the cell floor; his eyes still closed. He could tell that Gren was asleep by her breathing. He was furious with himself. She had come to him for help and he had let her down. He knew he wasn't really at fault; he had been dreaming. How many times had he dreamed that she'd appeared to him? He'd stopped counting orbits ago. He had to find a way to make it up to her.

Concentrating, Lawson tried to wander into Gren's dream. The fact that she had already given him permission didn't help appease his guilt. Staying very still, without speaking; he tried to make contact. A couple of times he made it to the edge of her dream, but he could never fully wander in. Why was it so much easier in a clinical setting, with the help of sleep tonic? Maybe he just needed to keep trying. Once he almost made it, but then it was gone. Had it been this hard for Gren? He tried again; failing to notice that Gren's breathing had changed. She was waking up.

"Lawson?" Gren called almost instinctively.

"I'm here, Gren."

Gren sat up. "I can't believe I fell asleep."

"You needed the rest."

"I wonder how long we've been here."

Lawson shook his head and sat up, as well. "I have no idea."

In a room on the far side of the ship, Captain Fia stood next to Handy, watching a monitor. "She's good," Fia commented. "No matter how hard she tried to hide it, I'm pretty sure that Gren was able to wander Lawson's dream. He wasn't quite as successful. He should have remembered what he learned as a White: scrunching up your face doesn't help you make it into a dream."

"Have ya noticed how protective he is of Gren?" Handy remarked. "We can use that."

"Oh, believe me...we will." Fia's smile grew. "A talented Dream Wanderer and an overprotective partner. This plan is *really* shaping up. I wonder if Gren is just as overprotective of Lawson."

"I say it's time we found out," Handy suggested.

"Patience," Fia said, holding up a hand. "The time will come."

Chapter Eleven

Staring at Roy's uniform, everyone was silent for several micros. Sham remembered seeing the symbol on a couple of objects at Roy's house when he was younger, but he always thought that all the talk of Abacu was just the ravings of a harmless madman. Maybe Roy really *was* insane, insane enough to make his own military uniform. No, Sham doubted that. There was life on other planets, and someone from Abacu had kidnapped Lawson and Gren.

Tayo shook her head, not fully believing what was going on. "What would the Royal Abacuan Army want with Gren and Lawson?"

Calli was trying hard to put the pieces together. "Gren's the best wandering student in her orbit."

"Hey!" Titus objected.

Calli ignored him. "And everyone knows that Lawson would do anything for her."

"Don't ya forget the missin' sleep tonic," Roy added.

"I still don't get it," Tayo said. "So there's some tonic and a couple of wandering students missing. What does this have to do with some army?"

Roy sighed. "As I'm sure they've told ya, sleep wanderin' is more than just a job; it's a big responsibility. It can affect people's thoughts and actions, especially if they don't know they're bein' wandered. That's why there are so many rules and laws, and why it's always done in a clinical settin'."

"Do you think the army wants them to wander someone's dream?" Sham asked.

"I have no idea," was Roy replied.

"So what do we do next?"

Roy stared at Sham for a micro. "Why are ya askin' me?"

Sham was slightly embarrassed by his assumption. "I don't know where else to turn. If you don't help . . . I don't know how we'll ever find them."

"So I'm supposed to risk my neck for a couple of kids I don't even know, and for one who's been too full of himself to come around and see me for the past several orbits?"

"Roy, I... I'm sorry," Sham stammered. "I . . ."

"I'm just teasin' ya," Roy said with a smile. "Follow me." He started to walk toward the back of the dwelling, the four students right behind.

Much to Tayo's dismay, Roy led them to the rundown building in the back. She was still having a hard time believing the scenario. Everyone else seemed to have bought it. "We're not really going in there, are we?" she asked as Roy fiddled with the controls by the door. She didn't think they would work. The overgrown weeds made it look like no one had entered in orbits.

"Have a little bit of faith in me, will ya?" The door opened quietly, not with a screeching noise as Tayo had expected. "Come on in."

Like the house, the inside of the smaller building didn't reflect the outside. It was one spotless area. Sitting in the middle was a vehicle of some type, unlike anything any of them had seen before. "What is it?" Titus asked, almost breathless.

"This," Roy said with pride, "is a PK-14. She's an older model, but I've taken good care of her. She'll get us to Abacu and back."

"Abacu?" the four friends repeated in unison.

"What did ya think? Ya can't save Gren and Lawson from here. Whose glidemobile is that?"

"It's mine," Calli said nervously.

"I'll need ya to co-pilot," Roy told her. "It's a long trip."

"I've never..." Calli objected.

"The controls are simple," Roy said. "If ya can handle a glidemobile, ya'll do fine. They're a lot alike."

"I want to help," Titus protested.

"Don't worry...there'll be plenty for everyone to do. I'll probably teach all of ya the controls. Are ya ready to go?"

"Now?" Tayo asked.

"Time's a-wastin'," Roy reminded them. He opened the door and walked into the PK-14. No one followed. "Are ya comin' or what?"

"Sham," Tayo said slowly, "I'm not so sure..."

Sham cut her off. "Fine, you stay here if you want to. But I'm going to find Lawson and Gren. Is anyone coming with us?"

"I'm in," Calli said, glancing back at her partner.

"Me too," Titus replied. The three of them entered the ship.

"Oh, all right," Tayo said, joining them. The door closed behind her. "I just think we're rushing into this. We haven't even tried to think of another plan."

"Ya got any ideas?" Roy asked, strapping himself into the pilot's chair. He motioned for Calli to sit in the seat next to his.

"No," Tayo said quietly.

"Then take a seat. I'd like for all of ya to stay up here durin' takeoff; it's a beautiful sight. Then I'll let Calli here take over the controls, and I'll show ya the rest of Puck."

"Puck?" Sham repeated.

"That's what I call her," Roy said with a proud grin. "Can't go around callin' her PK-14 all the time. Fasten yourselves in."

Everyone sat down and put on the safety straps. Roy pressed a button and the back wall of the building collapsed, revealing that it was really a door. Roy fiddled with a couple more controls, and the engines started. Calli looked at a total loss for what she was supposed to be doing. Roy turned around to those sitting behind him. "Ya might want to practice swallowin' real hard. It'll help make your ears pop. Or hold your nose and try to blow out through it. That also might help."

Tayo, who had never been much higher than a small hill asked, "Why?"

"Ya'll see soon enough." Roy took hold of a lever with his left hand, then pointed at something for Calli to his right. "Press that knob right there, real gentle-like."

Before anyone could say another word, Terra was far below them.

It didn't take Calli long to get the hang of Puck's controls. She was glad Roy could program almost everything; all she had to do was keep track of a few numbers and apply a small amount of pressure to one pedal. She had a feeling that even the pedal had been set by Roy, but he just wanted her to feel like she was doing something to help. "You're right," she told him, "the controls *are* very similar to a glidemobile."

"The modern glidemobile was designed by a joined couple from Abacu," Roy informed her. "Bet ya didn't know that."

"Wait a micro," Tayo said. "Are you telling us that there are other people from Abacu on Terra?"

Roy smiled. "Nah, there's no life on other planets. Come with me, I'll show ya the rest of Puck." He left the ship's cockpit, followed by Sham, Titus, and finally Tayo. Roy led them into a small room with a couple of chairs and a food service area on the side. "She's not very big, but she'll sleep four."

"Where?" Sham asked, looking around.

Roy smiled again and pulled open what looked like a drawer. It turned out to be a very small bed. "I didn't say she'd *comfortably* sleep four. With one person at the controls at all times, we'll be fine for the trip there, but it will be a little bit cramped once we find your friends. There's a necessary room in the back. Sorry, there's only one. I'm sure ya're used to boys' and girls' at that fancy school of yours."

"We'll be fine," Titus said.

"I hope so." Roy took a couple of steps back toward the cockpit. "Why don't ya get somethin' to eat, bring some up to the front as well, and then maybe think about gettin' some rest? Tayo, come with me. I'll go over the controls with ya. That way, no one has to worry about breakin' any Learning Center rules."

Sham protested. "We wouldn't..."

"I've known ya since ya were little," Roy reminded him. Sham shrugged his shoulders and didn't answer.

Chapter Twelve

After a night of very little sleep, Gren lay on her cot, her eyes still closed. "Lawson?" she called out quietly.

"I'm here, Gren."

"How did this happen?"

"I have no idea."

There were a million things Gren wanted to discuss with Lawson, but she was sure they were being watched. She would have to wait, try to wander his dream again. That was the only way she knew for sure they could communicate privately. Maybe after a while Lawson would take her seriously. She considered mentioning it, but she didn't want whoever might be listening to know she'd wandered his dream. In spite of their situation, Gren was rather pleased with herself. She had wandered farther into a dream than ever before. Hutch would be proud and furious at the same time...if only he knew.

"I didn't understand," Lawson said out of the blue, hoping that Gren would know what he was talking about.

"Yeah, I kind of figured that out." Gren was relieved that Lawson also thought they were being watched. She had been scared he would say something about her wandering. "It's no big deal."

"Do you think they'll give us anything to eat soon?" Part of Lawson was hoping that someone might be listening and take the hint.

"Is that all you ever think about?" Gren sat up on the small bed.

"It's easier to think about food than other things."

Gren wasn't sure if by "other things" he meant their current situation or the Learning Center's no-touch rule, but she didn't have a chance to ask him. Handy opened the cell door. He held the stick-weapon prominently in his hand. "Little girl, come with me."

Lawson sprang to his feet. "What about me? Gren's not going anywhere without me!"

"Ya think not?" He pointed the stick directly at Gren. "What do ya say now?"

"Lawson," Gren said nervously, "it will be fine. We have to do what he says."

"Listen to your girlfriend, here," Handy suggested. "If ya both do what we say, then maybe we'll look and see if we can't rustle ya up some grub. If ya don't listen..."

Handy motioned for Gren to move out of the cell. He locked it behind her, leaving his sentence unfinished.

They walked a different route than before. It was obvious that they were on a very large ship. Handy walked quickly; Gren was having a hard time keeping up. "Any chance we could slow it down just a little?" she pleaded.

"I just thought ya'd want to be back with your boyfriend as soon as possible," Handy said, dropping his pace slightly.

"He's not my boyfriend."

They walked silently for another hundred or so before Handy stopped abruptly. A door opened in front of them. "In ya go," he said.

Gren took a couple of steps forward and the door closed behind her, with Handy on the other side.

"Gren, how nice to see you again. I trust you slept well?"

Gren looked at Captain Fia, who was sitting at a table. "As well as can be expected."

"Please, my dear girl, have a seat." Captain Fia motioned, and Gren sat down. "Would you like anything? A cup of tea, perhaps?"

"No, thank you, ma'am."

"Ma'am?" Fia repeated with a smile. "Faking respect already? I didn't expect that quite so soon. Mind you, I did expect it sometime. You pretend to be coming around, pretend to have resigned yourself to my authority, hoping I'll lower my guard." She poured herself a drink from the pitcher in front of her. "How is Lawson? Hungry?"

"Why would you think he's hungry?" Gren asked. She hoped Captain Fia would admit that she and Lawson were being watched in the cell.

Captain Fia continued to smile as she poured Gren a cup of tea. "He's a man, my dear. Men are always hungry." She laughed once. "Well, he's *almost* a man." She took a long sip from her cup. "I suppose you're wondering why I brought you here."

Gren nodded. She stared at the cup in front of her. She was so thirsty! If there was something wrong with it, Captain Fia wouldn't be drinking it, would she? "Why am I here, but Lawson's not?"

"That will all be explained soon enough. We just need to set things up." Captain Fia pushed the cup toward Gren. "Drink it! It's just tea, I promise. You do realize that you'll have to start trusting me some time, at least a little bit."

Gren thought for a micro. Captain Fia was right. Until this was over, they rely on her for meals and other basic necessities. She lifted the cup and took a small sip. It tasted like any other tea she'd ever had. She took another sip. "It's good, thank you."

"All set, Captain." Handy's voice came out of nowhere.

"Thank you, Handy," Captain Fia replied into a small circle, which Gren guessed was a transmitter of some type. "Gren, I have a little favor to ask of you. Somewhere on this ship is someone who is asleep. They've taken some sleep tonic..."

"How did you get sleep tonic?" Gren interrupted.

"I have my ways," Fia said mysteriously. "I need you to find this person and wander their dream. Just for a hundred or two. And before you ask, they *have* given their permission, so you're not even breaking any wandering rules."

"I'm not allowed to wander outside of the Learning Center," Gren said sarcastically. "Without my license, it's illegal."

"Okay," Fia conceded, "so you're breaking *one* rule. But since we're not on Terra, we're not bound by their laws." She took another sip of her tea. "Just find the person, wander into their dream, and say to them, 'The sky is pink and the clouds are blue.' It's as simple as that."

"'The sky is pink and the clouds are blue'?" Gren repeated. "What kind of nonsense is that?"

"It's the code we're using so the person knows that they've been wandered," Fia explained. "Are you ready to begin?"

"No!" Gren's voice shook. "I'm *not* going to wander just because you tell me to!"

"I thought you might feel that way." Captain Fia flicked a switch, and a monitor illuminated before them. On the screen were Handy and Lawson. They were in a very small room. Gren guessed they weren't far from the cells. They couldn't be heard, which gave Gren a small amount of comfort; maybe her conversations with Lawson *weren't* being listened to. Lawson was seated. Handy stood behind him, the stick-weapon in full view. "Have you changed your mind?"

"No," Gren replied. "You're not going to kill Lawson. You

obviously brought us here for a reason, and my guess is that you need us alive."

"You're a bright girl. You're right, I'm not going to have Lawson killed. I don't kill children. But I do have the power to make things *very* uncomfortable for him. That chair he's sitting on? It's hooked up to an electrical charge. One zap and he'll be standing for several rotations. So, unless you'd like to see your partner jump *really* fast..."

"Okay," Gren said, defeated. "I'll do it."

"Make sure I can't tell that you're wandering," Fia instructed. She pressed a switch; Handy's and Lawson's images disappeared.

"Can I close my eyes?" Gren asked.

"Yes, but try not to move your mouth or anything like that. Are you comfortable enough?"

"I'm fine," Gren replied, gulping down more tea. She sat back, closed her eyes, and started to search. It was difficult. Someone could be asleep and not dreaming and Gren would never know, since she could only penetrate dreams. She continued to search. She had never tried to wander someone who wasn't right in front of her, but she'd learned about it in theory.

Suddenly, there she was. Gren saw a woman, walking alone down a long, dusty road. "The sky is pink and the clouds are blue," Gren said to her. Since that was all she'd been instructed to do, she left the dream immediately. She opened her eyes.

"Giving up so soon?" Captain Fia sounded annoyed. "Do I need to contact Handy?"

"No," Gren said quickly. "I did what you asked. I found the dreamer and gave her the message."

Fia's annoyance turned to excitement. "Her? You knew it

was a woman? What did she look like?"

Gren was slightly upset with herself; she hadn't paid much attention to the dreamer. She had just done as she'd been told. "Long, curly blond hair. I saw her from the back."

"What was the dream?" Fia wanted to know.

"She was walking down a road," Gren replied. "I didn't realize I was supposed to be observing her. It was a different sleep tonic than we use in our school lessons. I could tell that much, because it wasn't a nightmare."

"Hold on a micro." Captain Fia spoke into the transmitter again. "Bard, wake her up. Ask her if she received the message, and what was happening in the dream at that time."

"One micro, Captain." The silence was deafening. All Gren could think about was Lawson.

"Captain Fia," Bard's voice said, "she's awake. She got the right message, and she was walkin' alone on a dirt road."

"Thank you, Bard," Fia replied. She put down the circle. "Well done, Gren. Very well done. You and Lawson will be rewarded."

Less than a unit later, Gren and Lawson had both been returned to the cell. A large meal was set before them. They figured it was safe to talk about what had happened; anyone who might be listening would expect them to.

"Where did they take you?" Lawson asked, his mouth full of food.

"I met with Captain Fia. She wanted me to find someone and wander her dream...I think just to prove I could do it." She reached for another helping. She hadn't realized how hungry she was.

"And you did it?" Lawson sounded surprised.

"She said they would hurt you if I didn't," Gren told him.

"That chair they had you in...it was hooked up to some device. I could see you and Handy on a monitor. I . . . I couldn't chance it."

"I didn't know you cared," Lawson said with a grin.

"You have food on your face."

Handy stood once again at Captain Fia's side. The monitor was on, but watching Gren and Lawson eat didn't really interest either of them. "She wandered faster than we could have hoped or expected," Fia said. "She must be one of the best students in the history of that school."

"Ya think we need to test him as well?"

Fia thought. "Having two talented wanderers would be better than one. I'm just not sure he's up to the challenge. He didn't seem to do very well when Gren was sleeping."

"If he thinks she's in danger . . ."

"You're right. A little bit of pressure just might cause him to try harder. I'll see what I can think up." Fia clapped her hands once. "Overall, this has been a very productive session. Gren performed admirably. She also showed us she's willing to do what she's told to protect Lawson. A very good session indeed."

"And to think," Handy said with a grin, "there was nothin' hooked up to that chair at all."

"Fear can be a very powerful thing, my friend. Especially for our purposes. Fearing for themselves...and fearing for each other."

Chapter Thirteen

Roy and Calli sat in Puck's pilot's and co-pilot's chairs, talking. Tayo sulked behind them. She couldn't help but think they'd rushed into the trip. She worried about her family. What would they think when they found out she was missing? Would everyone assume they were helping Gren and Lawson? What if the cloth Sham found actually was a coincidence...what if Gren *had* run away with Lawson? Would she get kicked out of the Learning Center with just over one orbit left? If she couldn't become a licensed Dream Wanderer, what would she do with her life? She kept trying to tell herself that they were doing the right thing, but she was having a hard time being convincing.

"So how long have you lived on Terra?" Calli asked Roy.

"Oh, let me see, almost twenty-three orbits now."

"How did you end up there?"

"I was in the army for ten orbits," Roy said. "When I left, I moved to Terra. It seemed as good a place as any to start a new life. Lots of fresh clean air."

"Why didn't you want to stay on Abacu?"

"They don't really like it if ya leave the army," Roy said with a grin. "Besides, once ya see Abacu, ya'll understand. I had saved up enough money to buy Puck here, plus a little bit extra, so I left, and never even thought about goin' back. Until now, that is."

"What do you do on Terra?" Calli asked. "You know, for a job?"

"Odds and ends," Roy replied. "There's always someone need-in' somethin' fixed. I'm good at that type of thing. It's funny... Sham's parents won't let me anywhere near him, but I've fixed everythin' in his house from the front door to the necessary room equipment. Always, while he's been away at that Learnin' Center of yours, of course."

"I don't understand why they won't let him see you."

Roy glanced back at Tayo and smiled. "Because they think I'm flamin' nuts! Most Terrans do. When I first came to Terra, I tried to tell people about Abacu, tried to broaden their view of life. Turns out they don't want their views broadened. That's fine with me. If they want to think I'm crazy, then it's their loss, not mine."

Tayo suddenly broke her silence. "How long will it take us to get there?"

"About four rotations total."

"Four rotations!" Tayo exclaimed, outraged. "And then four more back?"

"Don't forget the time it'll take to find your friends," Roy reminded her.

"This is crazy," Tayo remarked, more to herself than anyone.

"We're off for a whole lunar cycle," Calli said sympathetically, "so if you're worried about school..."

"No," Tayo said, cutting her off.

"Then what are ya worried about?" Roy asked.

"We don't have a change of clothes," Tayo said, even though that was the last thing on her mind. "Eight plus rotations in the same uniform..."

"I've got some stuff in storage in the back," Roy told her.

"Thanks, but I really don't think your clothes would fit Calli and me," Tayo said sarcastically.

Roy shook his head. "I'm not talkin' *my* clothes. Some of my wife's stuff is still around here. It should fit ya just fine."

"Your wife?" Calli repeated. "I didn't know you were joined."

"I'm not anymore," Roy said sadly. "She died over twenty orbits ago."

○ ○ ◐ ● ◑ ○ ○

Sham and Titus were supposed to be sleeping in the other room, but they weren't doing a very good job. Titus was jealous that the girls had been taught the ship's controls.

Sham was just plain excited. He'd always enjoyed hearing about Roy's life; it was strangely gratifying to find out those stories were true. When they returned, he would tell his parents . . . no . . . he would tell the whole town that Roy wasn't crazy. He'd been telling the truth all along.

"They look pretty easy, don't you think?" Titus thought aloud.

Sham was confused. "What?"

"The controls!" Titus seemed surprised that Sham hadn't been thinking about the same thing he had. "I can handle a glidemobile."

"I don't know...you smashed up your dad's pretty bad a couple of breaks ago."

"That wasn't my fault," Titus retorted. "How was I supposed to know Dad had removed the pins from the main steering mechanism?"

"Maybe you could have asked him."

"Asked him if he'd removed the pins from the main steering mechanism?"

"No, you jerk," Sham said with a small laugh, "asked him if you could borrow the glidemobile!"

"Looking back on it, that might not have been such a bad idea," Titus agreed. "Hey, you're not going to tell Roy about that, are you? I would hate to think he wouldn't let me..."

"Relax," Sham assured his partner, "I won't mention it. So, what do you think it's going to be like?"

It was Titus's turn to ask, "What?"

"Abacu," Sham said happily. "Do you think it will look a lot like Terra? Or will the trees be covered with, I don't know, blue leaves with orange polka dots?"

"Who says the trees even have leaves?" Titus wondered.

"Or that they even have trees." Sham lay back on the small bed and put his hands behind his head. "This is so great...I can hardly wait."

"Except for the fact that our friends have been kidnapped."

"Oh. Yeah."

"I'm sorry," Calli said quietly. "I didn't mean to bring up any bad memories."

"It's fine," Roy said. "Ya didn't know. Besides, as I told ya, it was over twenty orbits ago. I've had some time to get used to the idea."

"What happened?" Tayo inquired, her attitude changing slightly. "If you don't mind my asking."

Roy shook his head. "We met on Abacu and were joined there, while I was still in the army. We had a couple of wonderful orbits together. We lived in Royal City, which is the capital, and where we're headed now. I was away on assignment and the city was attacked. The air became toxic for just a few hundreds, but she was out in it when it happened. She got real sick. I kept tryin' to get help for her, but no one seemed to care. It was about that time I decided to leave the army. We thought maybe the air would be cleaner somewhere else, and we ended up on Terra. It helped for a while, but then . . ." His voiced trailed off.

"What was her name?" Tayo asked softly.

"Breeze." Roy wiped a tear from his eye, then changed the subject. "My guess is they'll have a faster ship than we do. They'll probably beat us there by two rotations or more, dependin' on when they left. We'll need to come up with a plan."

"I'm open to suggestions," Calli said.

"How good at wanderin' dreams are ya?"

"We're just students," Tayo replied apprehensively. "Why?"

"Because there's no such thing as Dream Wanderers on Abacu," Roy explained. "We need to use any advantage we have. It's a big place. It's gonna to be hard findin' a couple of kids."

"We can assume they'll be with the army," Calli said.

"Maybe," Roy said, "but it's also a big army. The easiest place to start would probably be the Headquarters buildin'. I'll need all four of ya to tell me everythin' ya can about wanderin' so that maybe we can figure out why they wanted your friends and who they want them to wander. Tayo, come here."

"Why?"

"Calli, take my seat. Tayo, take Calli's. Ya remember all I told ya, right?" he asked Calli.

"I think so," Calli replied nervously.

"Good. I want ya to teach Tayo the co-pilot's duties. Everythin' is programmed. Ya just need to keep an eye on the numbers."

"Where are you going?" Calli asked.

"Back with the boys," Roy replied. "We're all gonna need to get some sleep sometime, and I have a feelin' they're not doin' much sleepin'."

"What if there's a problem?" Tayo asked, surprised to

suddenly have new, unwanted responsibilities.

"Then wake me up," Roy said, smiling. "Relax. Nothin' will go wrong. Puck can pretty much fly herself."

Less than a hundred later, Roy was in the back, pulling another bed out from the wall.

"What are you doing?" Sham asked.

Roy smiled. "I thought I told ya to get some sleep. And that's exactly what I'm plannin' on doin'."

"Sleep?" Titus repeated. "Then who is flying the ship?"

Roy dimmed the lights, knowing the boys wouldn't be able to see his grin. "I hope ya trust the girls...because our lives are in their hands."

"Oh, great," Sham mumbled.

Chapter Fourteen

It felt like time had stopped. Gren's nervousness lingered, but boredom had joined in, as well. She and Lawson both realized there were a great many things they couldn't talk openly about, in case someone was listening. More than anything, Gren wanted to go home. Part of her expected to hear Lawson's voice at any micro, telling her it was okay; it was just a dream. But it *wasn't* a dream; it was really happening.

Gren considered taking a nap and giving Lawson another chance to try wandering, but she didn't want to be too obvious. It didn't matter; she probably couldn't sleep, anyway.

"What do you think Sham told his parents?" Lawson asked. "I was supposed to spend my break with him."

"I thought Sham's parents were going to be away," Gren replied. "You and Sham were going to be on your own."

"That's true. I'd forgotten about that," Lawson said. "Sham was going to take me to meet an old friend of his, a friend who claimed he was from . . ." Lawson stopped.

"From where?" Gren asked. She didn't know whom or where Lawson was talking about.

"From another part of Terra," Lawson said quickly. "Used to live near the mountains. I always wondered what it would be like to climb one of those things."

Gren realized her mistake. Sham had spoken more than once about his "friend from Abacu." She also knew that Lawson had no desire whatsoever to climb a mountain. "Yeah, that would be interesting, to see the view from the top of the world."

Lawson knew she was mocking him, but he ignored it.

Whatever helped her feel better. "Sham and I would have had a great time. Not that I didn't enjoy having breaks with you...you know I did...but this would have been totally different. No rules, no authority, no one telling us what to do. Just two men enjoying no responsibilities."

"I don't know," Gren replied, imitating Sham's voice. "Two men? I think you both have a little way to go."

"Oh, be quiet," Lawson teased, smiling. He was pleased with himself. He had diminished Gren's fears, if only for a micro.

"Look at that, Handy," Captain Fia said, pointing at the monitor. "They're actually laughing. I think we need to turn up the fear factor a little bit, don't you?"

"Whatever ya say, ma'am."

"Bring them here," Fia ordered, "but take the long way. Make sure they get a glimpse of the Interrogation Room. Answer any questions they might have about it. But be vague on what is done there. Let them use their active little imaginations."

"Whatever ya say, ma'am," Handy repeated with a rotten-toothed grin.

A few hundreds later, Handy once again appeared at the cell door. "Both of ya, now," he said, menacingly pointing the stick.

All joviality was gone. Gren didn't even remember that she had been laughing not long before. More than anything, she wanted to reach out to Lawson and hold onto him, but she stayed back, mostly out of habit. "Where are we going?" she asked.

"Little girl, do ya have to ask that *every time* we leave?"

Gren couldn't remember having asked it before. "I'm sorry."

"This way," Handy said, pointing with the stick.

Lawson soon felt like they were walking just for the sake of it. He was sure there was no real destination. They were still on the same level as the cells. "Where *are* we going?" he asked at last.

"Oh," Handy groaned, "not *both* of ya! The two of ya truly are made for each other." He stopped in front of a heavy black door. Handy pushed it, and it opened a small amount with a loud creak. "Go ahead, take a peek."

First Gren, and then Lawson looked inside the room. It was dark and dusty, with several strange-looking items lined up along the walls. The place caused Gren to shiver. "Wh... wh... what is it?" she stammered.

"That's the Interrogation Room," Handy smirked. He seemed to derive a great amount of pleasure showing it to them.

"What's it for?" Lawson asked.

Handy rolled his eyes. "Interrogatin'. That's why it's called the *Interrogation Room*. A mighty useful place, if ya ask me."

"Who's it intended for?" Lawson asked, his voice cracking.

"Prisoners," Handy said casually. "There *is* a war on, ya know. 'Nuff about that. Get movin'."

Not long after, they went up several levels and entered yet another room on the ship. It was obviously someone's sleeping quarters. An elegant bed sat in the middle. It was canopied with opaque, multicolored cloth. There was a large window, curtained with the same type of material. The room had several soft, comfortable-looking chairs, a few other pieces of furniture, and a basin filled with water. The warm air smelled sweet, almost like a fruit dessert cooking.

Gren correctly guessed they were in Captain Fia's quarters. The woman appeared through a door in the back. Two men stood behind her. "Gren, Lawson, how nice it is to see you again. Please," she pointed to the basin of water, "feel free to wash up. I hate to say it, but you're both a bit on the filthy side."

Lawson took a step forward. "Well, if you didn't keep us locked up in that dirty..."

"How chivalrous," Fia said, ignoring his anger. "Making a stand for the girl of your dreams. Your dream *wanderings*, that is." She laughed at her joke.

Gren ignored the exchange and stuck her hands in the water. It felt good on her face. She rinsed herself off and, without asking, picked up a towel. "What do you want me to do this time?" she asked at last.

"Nothing," Fia replied. "I need nothing from you at all. It's Lawson's turn. In fact . . ." She turned to Handy. "Take Gren to the Interrogation Room."

Handy stepped between Lawson and Gren. "Whatever ya say, ma'am."

"No!" Lawson said quickly. A million thoughts ran through his mind. "Take me instead."

Captain Fia laughed. "Silly boy, this is a test of *your* abilities, not Gren's. But if you'd like her to stay and watch, I guess I can allow that. As long as you do what I ask of you."

"Anything," Lawson said feebly. "Just don't hurt Gren."

"Splendid." Captain Fia motioned to the men who'd entered when she had. "This test is really quite simple...not nearly as difficult as what I asked Gren to do. All three of us have bottles." She held one up, as did the two men. "Only one has sleep tonic. It's that quick-acting, light tonic, like they use during the Partnering Ceremony. We'll all pretend we're asleep. You have to wander to discover who is really having the dream. I'm one," she pointed, "he's two, and he's three. When you figure it out, just say the number. Then we'll wake the person up if we need to. Simple, right?"

Lawson nodded. "Just pop into the dream and say the number."

"That's right." Fia lay down on the bed. The two men sat in the chairs. "Drink up, boys." She lifted her own bottle to her lips.

Lawson tried to remember how long it took when Hutch drank the same tonic at the partnering ceremony. It seemed so long ago!

He counted to ten before starting to wander. It was obvious to him who would be having the dream. Captain Fia wanted to test his abilities. What better way than to take the tonic herself? Immediately he found himself inside her dream; it was much easier than what they had been doing in practice for orbits. Without moving his lips he let his presence he known by saying, "One."

He immediately left the dream. If Gren hadn't been threatened, he might have tried to suggest they be let go, but he wouldn't do anything to risk her safety.

"That was simple," Fia said, opening her eyes. She slowly sat up and yawned. "Gentlemen, please do what I asked." The two men stood and left the room.

"Well done, Lawson," Fia continued. She stifled another yawn. "I was sure you'd try to convince me to let you go, but you followed instructions instead. Gren, you can thank him for that, since *you* would have been punished. And since you did as you were told . . ."

She paused as the two men returned. They carried a bed between them. "For your reward, the two of you can spend the night here, instead of returning to that dirty old cell." She stood and motioned for the two men and Handy to follow her. "Your dinner will be brought to you soon. And just so you don't get any ideas, a guard will be posted outside."

"Wait," Lawson said quickly. "You said we don't have to return to the cells tonight. What about tomorrow?"

"Tomorrow," Fia said with a grin, "we arrive on Abacu."

For several micros, Gren and Lawson stared at each other. "What happened here?" Gren asked at last.

"I'm not sure," Lawson replied, "but I'm not complaining." He hopped onto the extra bed. "This sure beats sleeping on the floor."

"We arrive on Abacu tomorrow?" Gren repeated. "What happens then?" Fear filled her voice.

"Gren, my partner and my best friend," Lawson said, "I think we need to take things one micro at a time."

Back in her office, Captain Fia continued to smile. "We have them right where we want them," she told Handy. "As I've said before, fear is a very powerful thing."

"So he did okay, then?" Handy asked.

"He proved he'll do anything for Gren," Fia replied. "That's what I needed to know. It was a simple test, *too* simple...he's way past the abilities it required. But the best part, Handy, is that Gren showed up in the dream before Lawson did. The test was for her as well. She's willing to skirt around the edge of the law, but since I had given permission to be wandered, she technically didn't break it. Did she look any different?" Handy shook his head. "If I hadn't been expecting her, I never would have known she was there."

"And that's a good thing?" Handy asked.

"Someone who can observe quietly? Yes, my friend, that's a very good thing." She continued to smile. "Gren is an extremely talented Dream Wanderer. Fear and talent. What a wonderful combination. Ironic that none of our 'tests' has anything to do with what I'll actually require of them."

"So ya know how we're gonna use them?"

Fia paused. "I'm waiting for final instructions, of course, but I'm pretty sure I know what needs to be done."

Chapter Fifteen

After a few useless units, Titus gave up on the idea of trying to sleep. All he could think about was learning Puck's controls. He kept glancing at the timekeeper on the wall, sure that it must be wrong. He reasoned that, without a sunrise or sunset, time wouldn't seem normal. Still, it seemed to be moving awfully slowly. Sham's snoring wasn't helping matters any. As partners and roommates, Titus *should* be used to it by now. He usually didn't notice it anymore, but the adrenaline of being in space, the worries about his missing friends, and his outright jealousy and fear of the girls piloting the ship made him painfully aware of Sham's sounds.

His eyes having adjusted to the dim light, Titus glanced around. Roy seemed to be peacefully sleeping, as well. At least *Roy* could do it quietly.

A small noise and some light from the cockpit made Titus jump. Calli walked in, holding a small flashlight. "What are you doing?" Titus whispered loudly.

It was Calli's turn to be startled. She dropped the light, which went rolling across the floor. "You're supposed to be asleep," she whispered back.

"And you're supposed to be flying the ship."

"I have to use the necessary room," Calli retorted. "Not that it's any of your business."

"So who's flying...?"

Calli grinned, hoping Titus could see her. "Tayo is. She's never even flown a glidemobile, but now she's in control of Puck."

Titus sat up. "This is crazy! I'm going to go up there and..."

"Relax," Calli said, her voice calming. "It's all set on automatic. We haven't been doing much of *anything*. Just watching the readouts for fluctuations...of which there haven't been any."

"Oh." Titus lay down again.

"Don't worry." Roy's voice came from across the room. "Ya'll get your chance, Titus. Now go to sleep."

Calli picked up the flashlight and glanced at Sham. "Does he always snore like that?"

Titus shook his head. "No," he replied. "Sometimes he's a lot worse."

Two units later, everyone was awake. Calli and Tayo both looked tired. So did Titus, who'd never managed to fall asleep. Sham brought some food into the cockpit. The prepackaged food was tasteless and bland, the opposite of the feasts they'd grown used to at the Learning Center.

"Eat up," Roy encouraged everyone. He had once again taken the pilot's chair. "If ya don't, ya'll regret it later."

"I think I'm regretting it now," Titus whispered to Sham.

"I know it's not the best tastin' stuff that ya've ever eaten," Roy continued, "but it's nutritionally sound. It'll give ya energy. Believe me...once we make it to Abacu, energy is one thing that ya'll need."

"What else will we need?" Sham asked.

"I don't know," Roy replied. "I guess we'll find out when we get there. Calli, Tayo, it's your turn to get some sleep. Don't waste it, like one of the boys did." He glanced at Titus.

"We won't," Calli said. She and her partner walked out the door. "Good night, everybody."

Without being asked, Titus slipped into the co-pilot's chair.

"Okay, now what do you need me to do? What is this lever for?"

"Don't touch anythin'!" Roy shouted. "She's all set on automatic. For now, just keep an eye on the controls."

"So I don't get to actually fly her?" Titus sounded extremely disappointed.

"In time," Roy replied. "Which is something we currently have a whole lot of. Sham, I've known ya longer, and your friend seems a little impatient. Do ya want to learn the controls first?"

"I don't know," Sham responded. "Titus has been looking forward to learning more about Puck. I think we have only a few more micros until he bursts from frustration."

"Oh," Roy said with a grin, "that would make such a mess. Can't have his brain splattered all over the inside of my ship. Now, Titus, see that circular instrument over there? That needs to stay between 125 and 140."

It was Calli's and Tayo's turn to try to fall asleep. "Tell me what's going on," Calli implored her partner. "I know something's wrong."

"I just think we rushed into things," Tayo replied. "I mean, one hundred we're visiting an old friend of Sham's, the next we're in a spaceship, flying across the galaxy...to some planet I've never even thought much about...to rescue Gren and Lawson. It's too much to comprehend."

"I know what you mean," Calli said comfortingly, "but don't you think it's also exciting? Just a little bit?"

"No, I don't." Tayo paused. "Calli...I'm scared."

"Roy's not going to let anything bad happen," Calli promised.

"How do you know?" What do we even know about Roy?

Sham *used* to know him, but that was *orbits* ago. His family won't let Sham near him, and I can't help but wonder why."

"He already told us," Calli reminded her. "You know as well as I do...most people on Terra don't believe in life on other planets. That includes Sham's parents. What people don't understand, they tend to put down."

"Sham's parents think he's crazy," Tayo said. "What if they're right? What if we've just entrusted our lives to someone who..."

"Don't go there." Calli was growing angry. "There's nothing wrong with Roy. He was willing to drop everything to help us. You have to learn to trust people sometime."

"That didn't seem strange, either?" Tayo shot back. "He could just pick up and leave on a micro's notice? And that's an awfully big piece of land he owns for someone who makes a living doing odd jobs."

"You don't know if Roy owns the property," Calli said. "You always jump to conclusions. Man, it's no wonder you've had three previous partners. Trust is a very important part of the partnering relationship, and you obviously don't know how to trust anyone!"

"Don't throw that back at me," Tayo retorted. "I may have had three previous partners, but you've had four! Four different people released from the program, because they couldn't live up to your impossibly high standards! Two of my previous partners are still at the Learning Center. Yours are all no doubt having to have their own dreams wandered!"

"Why you..." Calli rose from her bed and took a step toward Tayo.

The cockpit door opened. "Would you two keep it down?" Sham said. "This door is supposed to be soundproof, and we can *still* hear you."

"Could you hear what we were saying?" Calli asked, embarrassed.

"No." Sham grinned. "Why, were you talking about me?"

"Good night, Sham." Calli watched the door close, then lay down once again on the small bed. She turned on her side and pulled the covers over her head. The sound of Tayo's breathing was too much to bear. Without either of them saying another word, the two Greens fell asleep.

Chapter Sixteen

With a stretch and a yawn, Gren sat up. She looked around, taking a micro to realize where she was. She didn't remember falling asleep. She remembered the dinner, talking with Lawson for a little while, and then growing tired. She vaguely recalled trying to stay awake so she could wander Lawson's dream again, but that was it. She didn't even know if she'd dreamed.

A loud groan indicated that Lawson was waking up. "Gren?"

"I'm here."

"Man, I slept well. It must be sleeping in a real bed. Sleeping on the cold, hard floor the way I have been..."

"By your own choice," Gren reminded him. "You could have returned to the other cell."

"True. But still, I feel really good right now. I haven't felt this rested since they threatened to break up our partnership."

"I know what you mean," Gren said. "I couldn't sleep very well once they started to talk about that, either." She thought back to dinner the night before. "Do you think that maybe the food...?"

"I think we were both totally exhausted," Lawson interrupted. "We were given a comfortable place to sleep, and our bodies took advantage of it. What you're thinking . . . I highly doubt it. I did some research about that sort of thing not too long ago, and there would have been side effects."

"When did you ever do research on 'that sort of thing'?" Gren half-asked, half-teased.

"When they threatened to break us up," Lawson replied. "Not being allowed to hang out with you...I've had a lot of free time."

"So you read about...?"

"I was plotting revenge," Lawson said with a grin. "I wouldn't have actually done anything, but it helped to think about it."

"Just when I thought I knew everything about you."

"Gren," Lawson said, "you should know by now that I'm full of surprises."

"You're full of *something*, all right," Gren joked. She remained silent for a micro. "Captain Fia said we're arriving on Abacu before the end of the rotation. What do you think will happen to us?"

"As long as we do what they ask, we'll be fine," Lawson tried to assure her. "They've proven that to us so far. We just need to stick together. Be brave, Gren. We can do it."

The door opened. Captain Fia and Handy walked in. "Good, you're awake," Fia said. "I hope you slept well." Gren glanced at Lawson but didn't say anything. "It's a busy, busy rotation, so you'd better get up and get going. I'd advise you to take advantage of the bathing area while you can. One at a time, of course. Oh, and I almost forgot. There are fresh clothes for you in that cabinet over there." She pointed across the room.

"Why can't we just wear our uniforms?" Lawson asked. He hadn't worn anything other than a Learning Center uniform since he was a White.

"No offense, Lawson, but your uniform...well, let's just say it could use a good washing," Fia told him. "Disinfecting, as well. And I need you to fit in, which you won't if you're looking like a giant piece of the sky. Although blue skies are rare where we're headed.

"So hurry now, you have half of a unit. Handy will be outside the door waiting for you. If you're not ready on time, he'll bring you, anyway." Handy didn't say a word, just smiled menacingly. "Believe me, you won't want to miss what I have in store for you." She and Handy left, closing the door behind them.

⋄ ◦ ⦿⦿◦ ◦ ⋄

It didn't take long for them to get ready, but Gren and Lawson decided to let Handy come for them, anyway. After exactly half a unit, he opened the door and pointed the ever-present stick weapon at them. Neither of them resisted.

Handy led them to the same control room where they had first met Captain Fia. Not being quite as nervous or confused as the last time they were there, Lawson paid more attention. He was pretty sure they were in the bridge area.

Captain Fia stood nearby. She smiled when she saw them. "Don't you feel better now? Clean hair, clean clothes . . ."

"I don't like these clothes," Gren said boldly, remembering what Lawson had said about being brave. She glanced down at herself. She was wearing a ragged, baggy brown dress with a rope belt. Lawson was dressed in a gray shirt and black pants with holes in both knees. They both wore sandals.

"I don't care *what* you like or don't like," Fia said sternly. She took a step closer. "What you need to understand, Gren, is that you will do what I want you to do, wear what want you to wear, eat what I want you to eat, drink what I want you to drink, say what I want you to say, think what I want you to think. *I'm* currently in control of your life, not you. We'll all be happier when both of you realize that."

She smiled. "And when I'm done with you, after you've

finished what I need you for, you'll be returned home, happy, healthy, and safe."

"What if we don't do what you want?" Lawson asked.

"That's why we brought both of ya along," Handy reminded them. "If one of ya doesn't behave, your partner pays the price."

"Come, have a bite to eat," Fia said cheerfully, purposely changing the subject. She put an arm behind Gren and nudged her forward. "The pastries are divine." She led them to a couple of seats and motioned for them to sit down. They had a good view out the large window.

Gren and Lawson both received plates of food. Lawson started to eat hungrily, as always. Gren picked up a pastry and took a bite.

"Good girl," Fia commented. She took a seat, as well.

"Countdown has begun. We're at approximately five hundreds," a worker called.

"Keep me informed," Fia replied, sounding businesslike. She returned her attention to Gren and Lawson. "I suppose you're wondering, countdown to what."

"Only if you want me to," Gren replied bitterly.

"Drop the attitude, Gren," Fia ordered. "I can always have Handy return you both to the cells. Or better yet . . . Handy?"

"No," Gren said quickly. "I'm sorry. Um, countdown to what?"

"To our entrance into the Abacuan atmosphere," Fia told them. "Keep watching. We should be getting a glimpse of the planet soon."

Soon, a large ball appeared in the window. Swirls of blue and white were everywhere. Lawson took a deep breath and wondered, just for a moment, if maybe their kidnapping had been worth it after all. The planet grew closer and closer. As it continued to grow, a new color appeared: a small grayish area. "What's that?" Lawson asked. "It looks weird."

"You've got good eyes," Fia told him. "That, my dear Lawson, is Royal City. It also happens to be where we're headed."

"Why?" Gren asked. Then she added, "Ma'am."

"I'll give you credit for trying," Fia chuckled, "but I have to admit, I thought Lawson would be the one giving me a hard time. Let me give you a little bit of background. If you haven't figured it out already, we're members of the Royal Abacuan Army. We've been at war with the planet Eden for going on fifty orbits. Their leader, Ivan the Fourth, decided it wasn't enough to oppress his own people...he went after us, as well. He's turned our once beautiful planet into . . ." Fia wiped a tear from her eye. "But it's all going to be over soon. The war, the oppression...everything."

"We're entering the atmosphere in five . . ." the worker started.

Everyone on the bridge joined in. "Four . . . three . . . two . . . one."

Except for a momentary, slight shaking, entering the atmosphere didn't feel any different. Lawson had expected to feel like the ship was breaking apart. The change outside the window was evident, but inside it was almost like nothing had happened. "This ship is top of the line," Fia explained, seeing the confusion on Lawson's face. "She's *made* for reentry. Believe me, it wasn't always this pleasant. She has stabilizers and sensors to detect changes in pressure and gravity and the like. Just sit back and enjoy the view. Most Terrans will never have this opportunity."

Except for the sound of people working the controls, the

bridge was silent. Neither Gren nor Lawson spoke, out of sheer amazement. Finally, a worker said, "We've been given permission to land, ma'am."

"Good," Fia replied. "Gren, Lawson, you're about to help bring peace to my world."

Chapter Seventeen

L anding was uneventful. The ship touched ground with a slight bump. Besides a dirty, grayish wall, Lawson couldn't see a thing through the window. Something hummed overhead and the light slowly dimmed; Lawson guessed there was a retractable roof.

"All clear, Captain," said the man who appeared to be the pilot.

"Good," Fia replied. "Handy?" She snapped her fingers and pointed at Gren and Lawson.

"Whatever ya say, ma'am." Handy approached Gren, a long piece of rope in his hands. "Hands in front, little girl, wrists together. Don't look so scared...I won't hurt ya."

Gren looked terrified. "I promise, Captain Fia, ma'am, we won't try to run away. We'd have nowhere to go, no way to get home . . ."

"Relax," Fia said, a calming quality to her voice. "It's just for show. We can't draw attention to ourselves. You're dressed as slave children; we need to finish the look. You'll be untied as soon as we reach our destination. You have my word."

Lawson wasn't sure if he could take his kidnapper at her word, but he decided not to call her on it. Instead, he asked a question: "There are slaves on Abacu?"

"Not really slaves, per se," Fia replied. "There are no labor camps, like there are on Terra. When someone is convicted of a crime, they're sentenced to what we call 'slave time.' They're assigned a place to serve out their time, often within the military."

"Even children?" Gren asked.

"Royal City is a hard place to live," Fia said sadly. "There's a lot of poverty. Children sometimes break a law, *hoping* to receive slave time. They know they'll at least be given meals and a warm place to sleep. Now enough stalling. Do as Handy said."

Gren, visibly shaking, held her hands in front of her and allowed her wrists to be tied. A long piece of rope hung down from her wrists. Handy repeated the process with Lawson.

"Sometimes, in a case like this, the two of you would be tied together," Fia said, "but that would break your 'no physical contact' rule, so we'll do it this way. See? I can be reasonable." She reached over and tousled Gren's hair. "There, that's better. You truly look like you belong here. Come on."

Lawson had been right. The ship had landed in a docking bay, and the roof had closed over the top of it. As they took their first steps outside the ship, Gren remembered that Fia had said the gravity on Abacu was stronger than on Terra. It didn't feel all that different, or maybe she had just grown used to it on the ship.

Fia took hold of the rope binding Gren, Handy did the same with Lawson's, and the four of them walked toward a door. The rest of the ship's crew stayed behind. "Keep your heads down," Fia advised. "Don't be looking around. Slave children would already know what the city looks like. And they wouldn't talk in public, so don't say a word."

She opened the door, and they went outside. Gren stared at her feet, but Lawson couldn't resist trying to look out of the corners of his eyes. What struck him immediately was that everything was a dingy gray. The buildings appeared to be made of stone; the street was made of mud. There was a cold, light rain falling, making it easier to not look up.

"Nice rotation," Handy commented.

Both Gren and Lawson thought he was being sarcastic until Fia replied, "That it is. This is the lightest rain I've seen here in a long time."

"I'm surprised there aren't more people out enjoyin' the weather."

Still looking peripherally, Lawson observed that there were just a few people outside. He noticed one other army uniform; the rest of the people seemed to be dressed in rags. They were in an obviously poor area. The few vehicles they'd seen all bore the army's symbol.

After a walk of a few hundreds, they stopped and waited. A small number of people joined them. There were mumblings about the 'slave children,' but neither partner said anything. They just kept their heads down. Soon a vehicle resembling a large glidemobile stopped. Lawson bit his tongue to keep from asking. They were led on, and the four of them took seats in the back.

"If it becomes too crowded you and Lawson will be expected to give up your seats," Fia whispered to Gren. "But I doubt it will happen. It's not a long ride."

At the front of the vehicle, two more children, hands tied to each other, boarded. They were also led by members of the Royal Abacuan Army. They kept their heads down, reminding Gren and Lawson to do the same. Soon the vehicle sped away. It was moving so fast that everything outside became a blur, although there was little to see. Dirty gray continued to be the predominant color. The vehicle stopped twice to let passengers off and pick up others. The third time it stopped, Fia and Handy both stood, causing Gren and Lawson to do the same. "Come!"

Fia ordered, pulling on the rope. They were the only ones to exit the vehicle.

There was another drizzly walk, this time up a hill. Both Blues were soon breathing hard, as was Handy. Captain Fia acted as if she could walk uphill forever. When they reached the top, they walked through a barrier made of trees. The trees were disappointing; they looked like anything that could be found on Terra.

Although they weren't supposed to look around, neither Gren nor Lawson could help looking up at the building suddenly in front of them. It was taller than any structure they'd ever seen...at least twenty stories high. Even more striking was the shiny purple exterior. "Impressive, isn't it?" Fia asked. "And you can drop the charade now. Even slaves can't help but stare when they first see it."

"What is it?" Lawson asked.

"Military headquarters," Fia replied. "I've never been able to understand the logic of making it stand out quite so much, especially in a time of war, but it's constructed of some of the strongest material available. So far, it's made it through the war unscathed."

"How tall is it?" Lawson asked.

Fia smiled. "I forgot. You're used to the low buildings at the Learning Center. Twenty-three stories high, although we won't be going into most of them. We'll be going right to the top. That's where you can do what I need you for."

"What *do* you need us for?" Gren asked.

"I told ya," Handy said, looking at Captain Fia, "she's an impatient one."

"Patience is one of the most valuable things to strive for, my dear Gren," Fia said. "You'll know your purpose here soon enough."

"I thought you were going to untie us when we got here," Lawson reminded Fia.

"When we're settled in," Fia said. "What I just said to Gren about patience? Well, Lawson, consider it your lesson too. And before we enter, I want to remind you both of one thing."

"What?" they asked in unison.

"If you do what is asked, you'll be rewarded. If not..." Captain Fia let her words drop.

Chapter Eighteen

Murmurs sounded around them as the foursome entered the building. Ignoring everyone, Captain Fia led them to a lift.

They were soon speeding up, faster than either Blue had expected. They stopped and exited into a large, open room. Two walls were made completely of purple-tinted windows. As promised, both Gren and Lawson were immediately untied. Gren rubbed her wrists; even though the rope hadn't been tight, she had grown sore.

A woman approached them, staring at the partners. "Is this them?" she asked Fia excitedly.

Handy mumbled something under his breath while Fia replied, "Yes, our mission was a complete success. Gren is the finest student I've ever seen, and Lawson...well, he shows some promise, too."

"I'll inform the General," the woman said. She disappeared down a hall.

"'Is this them?'" Handy mocked. "Just who did she think they were?"

"Handy . . ." Fia warned. Handy didn't say another word but continued to mumble. "Gren, Lawson, come over here," Fia said. She approached a window. "There's something I want you to see."

Without having to be asked twice, they joined Fia. The view was spectacular. The sky was still a dingy gray, but some of the dinginess seemed to be clinging to the ground. Looking out of the window, they could see some of the city's buildings. "Is that where we just came from?" Lawson asked.

"We came farther than that," Fia told him, "but yes, from that direction. Now, look over here." She took them around a corner to the other window. "The city is surrounded almost entirely by a wall," she explained, pointing.

"What's that over there?" Gren asked. Beyond the wall was mostly forest, but one large area had been somewhat cleared. It was hard to make out, but it looked like there were dwellings. There were also several similar, smaller areas.

"That's why we brought you here," Fia said.

A noise came from behind them: someone clearing his throat. Fia turned around quickly. "General, sir," she said with respect. "These are the Dream Wandering students I promised I'd bring here."

The General was extremely tall and muscular, with the sternest look imaginable on his face. He walked around Gren, looking her over. He then did the same thing with Lawson. When he was done with his inspection, he turned his attention to Fia. "A boy and a girl? From what ya said, I didn't think that was allowed."

"No, sir," Fia replied, "it happens sometimes. These two have been together all the way through the program. Their bond is very strong. This is Gren and..."

The General cut her off. "I don't care to know who they are... just if they can do the job."

"Yes, sir," Fia assured him. "I have complete confidence in her abilities." She didn't mention Lawson. "And as I said, their bond is very strong."

"Do they know why they're here?" the General asked.

"Not yet, sir."

"Isolate them," the General ordered. "Show them where

they'll be stayin'. Keep them apart, and explain to them individually what ya need them to do. Eventually. Ya don't have to tell them anythin' yet."

"Yes, sir."

"This is *your* project, Captain," the General snapped. "It had better work."

"It will, sir," Fia replied.

◦ ◦ ◦ ● ◦ ◦ ◦

A few hundreds later, Gren was being led down the hallway by Captain Fia. Handy and Lawson had gone off somewhere else. "Please," Gren begged, "we've done everything you've asked. Please don't separate us."

"I'm following orders," Fia said. "I'm sure you can understand that. We're going to ask a lot more...especially of you, Gren."

They stopped in front of a door. Fia typed in a code and it opened. "In," she said. The room was tiny. A bed hanging from the wall was the only furnishing. In the back, an open door led to a necessary room.

"Sit." Gren sat on the bed and continued to rub her wrists. Fia closed the door and sat down next to her. Her voice calmed. "Gren, it's not all that bad. You'll be well taken care of while you're here. I'll admit your accommodations are a little bit boring, but it won't be for long. We'll have you back in plenty of time to enjoy the last few rotations of your break."

"What is it you want me to do?" Gren asked. She was trying hard to not cry.

"Just a little bit of wandering," Fia replied. "Trust me; you're perfect for this job."

"Trust you!" Gren repeated. "*Trust* you? After you dragged us away from our home?"

"You're going to have to trust someone," Fia said. "It might as well be me, since I have the power to get you back to that very same home. And as I said, it's just a little bit of wandering."

Gren looked Fia straight in the eyes. "What if I refuse?"

Fia stood up. "That," she said, stepping toward the door, "would make Lawson very unhappy." She typed in her code and the door opened. "Think about it."

As soon as the door closed again, the tears started to flow. Gren lay down and buried her face in the bed. She had never felt so alone or cried so hard. She didn't know if she would ever stop.

"Hey, Gren!"

Gren looked around as soon as she heard Lawson's voice. She didn't see him. Somehow, the room had reduced to half its size. She sat up on the bed, which shrank under her. "Lawson, where are you?" Gren was panicking. "I can't see you."

"Of course you can't," Lawson calmly replied. "I'm wandering your dream. I actually did it, Gren! No tonic or anything. Aren't you proud of me?"

"You're wandering?" Gren repeated. "So none of this is real?"

"No, it's real. But it looks like you've shrunk everything. Stand up in the middle of the room and put your arms out as far as you can."

Gren did as she was told. Her arms were bent; she felt as if the walls were closing in on her.

"Now, place your hands against the walls and push!" Lawson commanded. "Push the walls as hard as you can, until your fingers can barely touch them at the same time. Then your room will be the right size, you'll have overcome your fear, and we can talk."

Wanting to talk to Lawson more than anything, Gren pushed with all her strength. The walls moved easily, and soon the room resembled reality. She sat down. "How did you know I'd be sleeping?"

Lawson sighed. "Gren, this is me. I know you better than anyone. After Fia locked you in there, you cried yourself to sleep. At least, I thought you probably would. I figured it was worth a shot. So what did Fia tell you?"

Gren thought for a micro. How she wished she could see Lawson instead of only hearing his voice. "That she's going to need me to wander. And if I don't, *you'll* be sorry."

"Did she say who she wants you to wander?"

"No, but I figure it has something to do with those clearings in the woods."

"You think?" Lawson teased. "Fia said that's why we're here."

"Oh, yeah," Gren said, embarrassed. "I knew I'd heard that somewhere. What did Handy say to you?"

"Not much of anything. He mentioned that I need to sit tight, and he said something about the end of the war."

"Who could Fia want me to wander?" Gren wondered. "And what does that have to do with this war they keep talking about?"

"That's it!" Lawson exclaimed. "They want you to wander someone from the other side...get information from them. Then the General will be able to attack because he knows their plans."

"Why would they tell me anything?" Gren asked. "Especially in a dream."

"Remember what Hutch always told us? Dream Wanders have power. They can manipulate dreams to find out what they want." Lawson mocked Hutch's voice. "'That's why you need a license.' Come on, Gren, it fits."

"So the deaths of hundreds, maybe thousands, of people will be on our heads?" Gren's voice was filled with fear.

"Not if you don't do it."

"But they'll hurt you!"

"Give them false information," Lawson suggested. "Let's both try to find out as much as we can about the war. We'll share what we learn in our dreams. And they're not going to hurt me. They need both of us to keep the threats going."

"Lawson, I'm scared."

"Hey, who's that coming toward you?" Lawson asked.

Gren squinted, looking at a shadowy figure. "Out of the necessary room?"

"Yeah, that's me!" Lawson exclaimed.

The dream-Lawson stepped forward then sat on the bed next to Gren. "We may not be allowed any physical contact in real life, but I'm just a dream, so I can hold you." He put his arms around her.

Gren was comforted, even though she knew it wasn't real. And even though he could only watch while wandering, the real Lawson was comforted, as well.

Chapter Nineteen

As each rotation passed, Puck's interior seemed to grow smaller. The idea of being in space had lost its thrill, and the close quarters were growing more annoying by the micro. Calli and Tayo especially were getting on each other's nerves.

The ship was still being flown in shifts, but the excitement was gone, since she pretty much flew herself. Calli sighed as she stared at the unchanging numbers on the instruments. "It probably won't be too much longer. I bet something will change soon."

"Yeah, right," Tayo replied. "I doubt we'll ever make it to Abacu. We'll probably be stuck here, flying around nowhere, until the food or oxygen runs out."

"Don't be such a pessimist," Calli snapped. "Roy knows what he's doing."

Tayo ignored her partner. She still didn't trust Roy. "I hope it's the oxygen. That sounds easier than starving to death."

"No one's gonna starve," Roy said as he entered the cockpit. Sham and Titus were right behind him. "At least not this orbit." They all sat down. "We're gettin' close; it should only be a couple more units."

"Yeah, right," Tayo mumbled again under her breath.

Roy grinned. He pointed at a bright light, which appeared to be growing larger. "Ya see that, right up ahead?" Everyone nodded. "That's Abacu. We'll be takin' Puck out of automatic in about a unit, so what ya need to do is formulate a plan."

"I don't know," Sham started. "What do *you* think we should do?"

Roy paused and glanced around. "Me? Why do ya think I know what to do?"

"You've been there before," Calli said.

"True," Roy replied. "But I know nothin' about wanderin'. That's what they wanted your friends for...it's got to be. What can ya tell me about it?"

"There's not all that much too it," Calli said. "Those of us who have the gift can enter someone's dream and guide them through it. Wandering's used a lot for children who have nightmares or for adults with anxiety problems."

"The Wanderer actually makes it into the dream?" Roy asked.

"Yeah," Sham replied. "The dreamer can't see us, but they can hear us, and we can see what's going on. It's pretty cool, but there are a lot of restrictions. The most important rule is that we have to have permission to wander."

"How long does it take?"

"Not long," Calli replied. "With sleep tonic, it can be done in a few hundreds."

"Who's the best Wanderer out of the four of ya?" Roy asked.

At first no one answered. "Calli and I are a rotation behind," Tayo said at last.

"Okay, that leaves the boys," Roy said. "Which one of ya is a better Wanderer?"

Titus took a deep breath and held up his finger, as if he was about to say something. He paused and slowly let the breath out. "Sham is," he said. It seemed like a difficult thing for him to admit.

"No one in our entire orbit is even close to Gren," Sham added. "Ladinda and Hutch have both told us they expect all of us to be as good as she is."

"Ladinda and Hutch?"

"Ladinda runs the Learning Center, and Hutch is one of our teachers," Calli said.

"Oh." Roy thought for a few micros. "So, Sham, could ya wander *my* dream? It would make it a lot easier for me to understand, and then maybe we can figure out what they want your friends for."

"I don't know . . ." Sham said nervously.

"We don't have any sleep tonic," Tayo pointed out.

"There's another way," Titus said. "Hutch taught us. It won't produce nightmares, but that's not needed for a demonstration. Roy, Sham, come with me." Titus stood and went back to the other area, with Roy and Sham following. He pulled out a bed. "Lie down and close your eyes." Roy did as he was told. "Take deep breaths, and imagine yourself the most comfortable you've ever been. All of life's difficulties have been washed away; all you have to do is drift off to sleep."

"You've never done this before," Sham whispered.

"And you've never wandered an adult before," Titus quietly shot back. "Relax," he continued, "and count slowly in your mind backward from a hundred. When you reach one, allow yourself to dream."

The partners watched as Roy seemed to drift off to sleep. Sham sat down and waited. He was nervous, but he wasn't sure why. A slight smile crossed Roy's face.

"Breeze, I'm home!" Roy was in his dwelling, but it was different. Everything seemed newer than when the four students had been there. It was filled with light. "Breeze? Where are ya?"

"She's . . .she's in another room," Sham started, his voice cracking.

"The bedroom?" Roy asked. His clothes were strange: a bright, multi-colored pattern that Sham recalled seeing in a history lesson. Roy didn't look any younger, but everything else suggested it was at least twenty orbits earlier.

"Yes, the bedroom," Sham replied. "Look for her in the bedroom." He had no idea whom Roy was looking for.

Roy walked quickly through the house. He seemed to be excited about something. "Breeze, I have great news!" he called. "Are ya in the bedroom, my love?"

Sham was taken aback for a micro. He had never thought of Roy as being in love with anyone. He had always pictured him as a recluse. "Who is Breeze?" he asked.

"She's my wife," Roy replied, annoyed to have to explain it. He entered the bedroom. A woman, at least twenty orbits younger than Roy, sat in a chair in a corner. She was wrapped in a blanket and not moving. Roy rushed over to her. "Breeze, are ya alright?"

"She's fine," Sham informed him. "She was just asleep."

Breeze stirred. "Sorry, I didn't hear ya come in. I guess I dozed off." She coughed violently.

"How are ya feelin'?" Roy asked.

"She's feeling better," Sham said, not sure what else to say.

"I'm feelin' better," Breeze replied. She reached up and touched Roy's face. "I always feel better when ya're around."

Roy bent and kissed his wife. Sham was slightly embarrassed to be watching. "Tell her your news," he reminded after several micros.

Roy pulled away. "I have good news. They're givin' me work I can do from here. I won't be leavin' ya all the time any more."

Breeze smiled, then coughed several more times. "That *is* good news." She coughed again.

Sham wasn't sure what else he should do. "You have more good news," he said at last.

"I do?" Roy was surprised.

"Yes," Sham replied with a little more confidence. "You've found a doctor, one who can help." He wasn't sure what was wrong with Breeze, but he wanted to turn the dream into something positive.

"I have?"

"Yes," Sham said more forcefully. "Tell her."

"Breeze, my love," Roy started, looking confused, "I've found a doctor. One who says he'll be able to help."

"It's too late for me," Breeze replied gently. "We both know that."

"No, it's not too late," Sham told Roy.

"No, it's not too late," Roy repeated.

Breeze coughed several more times. "Ya can't change history, my love. Not even in your dreams."

Roy opened his eyes and sat up. He sighed. "If only it was that easy, Sham. But that was interestin'. I think I have a better appreciation for what a Dream Wanderer does."

Sham sat down next to Roy. "Was she really your wife?"

Roy grinned. "Yeah. She died a long time ago. The girls could have told ya. They found out all about Breeze rotations ago."

"Breeze?" Titus, who hadn't been in on the dream, repeated.

"Sham will tell ya later," Roy said.

"The girls wouldn't have told us anything," Sham replied. "They've been too busy not getting along."

"Ya're right," Roy agreed. "Somehow, I don't think they're actin' much like partners right now." He decided to change back the subject. "So when ya wander, it's possible to suggest where to go and what to do?"

"Yeah," Sham said. "It's actually pretty easy. I think with you it was a little bit harder. I'm guessing that's because some form of your dream had really happened." Roy nodded. "But with the right type of sleep tonic, you can make suggestions, even manipulate a dream. They're always warning us about the power of the profession."

"Interestin'." Roy seemed to be lost in thought. "Since it's probably the army that took them..." The ship jerked hard, interrupting his sentence.

Calli poked her head in from the cockpit. "Roy, quick! It looks like we've got a problem."

Chapter Twenty

Gren was sure she'd been in the small cell for rotations, but she had no idea how many. She hadn't seen Captain Fia again. The only time she'd had any human contact at all was when someone brought food. At least, that was the only face-to-face contact. She spent every waking moment trying to wander Lawson's dreams.

They were both getting a lot of practice. Lawson had discovered, much to his delight, that he could place himself into a sleeplike state that was easy for Gren to wander. Because he was still partially conscious, he had some control over the dream, making communicating fairly easy. Gren enjoyed spending time in Lawson's dreams. She missed him more than she could have imagined.

Their attempts to find out about the war had failed miserably. The person who brought the food never said more than, "Here ya go!" The first few wanderings, Gren and Lawson argued about what to do once they finally discovered who she would be asked to wander. They soon decided that, instead of fighting, they should cherish their time in each other's dreams. Often, Lawson dreamed they were back by the lake at the Learning Center. At first, it bothered Gren how easy it was for Lawson to dream of breaking the rules, but the more she wandered, the less she minded.

"Remember when we were Whites?" Lawson asked. He was sitting in the sand, with Gren leaning against him. They were wearing their slave-children clothing instead of their uniforms.

"What about it?" The Gren in the dream wasn't the one who

answered. Lawson was getting used to the sensation of seeing one Gren but hearing another elsewhere.

Lawson smiled. "Remember how nervous we were around each other? I never told you this before, but I was *so* upset about being partnered with a girl!"

"You've told me that before. Like the last several times I wandered."

"Oh yeah, I keep forgetting this isn't really happening," Lawson said.

"If it were really happening, we'd be kicked out of the Learning Center."

"Yeah." Lawson shook his head. "Stupid rules."

Unexpectedly, Gren's door flew open and Captain Fia and Handy entered the room. "Gren," Fia said sternly. "Come."

"What's going on?" Lawson asked. He couldn't hear Fia, but he knew Gren's concentration had been interrupted.

Gren tried to make contact again without making it obvious. "Fia's here," she whispered into his dream without moving her lips. "I'll let you know what's going on as soon as I can."

"Gren," Fia said with a sigh, "I know what you two have been up to. Stop trying to send messages to Lawson. He's perfectly fine ...for now. So do as I say, and come with me."

A few hundreds later, the three of them waited for the lift. "Where are we going?" Gren asked nervously.

"Up," Fia simply replied.

"Up?" Gren repeated. "I thought we were on the top floor."

"We are." Fia offered no further explanation.

The door opened. "In ya go, little girl," Handy said.

The three of them entered the elevator. Even though she had been told, Gren was surprised that they went up. The door opened and they stepped out. Fia used a code, and another door opened. They walked out onto the roof. It was nighttime. The drizzle they'd encountered before was gone, but no stars were visible.

"See, Gren, I told you we were going up," Fia said with a smile. She put an arm around Gren and led her to the edge. A wall as high as Gren's shoulders enclosed the building's perimeter.

Handy stood to one side, conversing into a communicator. He then gave a signal to Captain Fia.

"See over there?" Fia pointed to the same cleared area they'd seen when they first arrived. "I have another little experiment for you. Someone there has taken some sleep tonic. He's normal height, with dark hair, a nice-looking guy. His name is Vomat; he's the camp's commander. Here's his picture." She handed Gren a small photo. "I want you to wander and give him a message."

"Wandering without permission is illegal," Gren said, mostly out of habit.

"Illegal on Terra," Fia replied, as if she'd expected the argument. "We're not *on* Terra, now, are we?"

"If it's not illegal, it's still immoral," Gren said quickly. "Dreams are supposed to be private and if I..."

"I'm not asking you to tell me what he's dreaming," Fia interrupted. "I just want you to give him a message. If you do, I'll let you see Lawson."

"But if ya don't . . ." Handy added.

"I can't wander that far away," Gren said quickly. "I've never tried."

"Then you don't know whether you can or can't," Fia said. "You're running out of excuses, my dear. What it comes down to is this: Would you like to see Lawson? Or would you rather have *him* pay for *your* stubbornness?"

Gren took a deep breath, thinking. "What's the message?"

Fia smiled again. "I knew you'd come around. It's very simple, really. Just tell him 'There will be an attack at dawn.'" Gren was horrified. "Don't look at me like that, Gren. You'll actually be helping everyone. If you were leading a campaign and were about to be attacked, wouldn't you want to know?"

"I guess," Gren replied feebly.

"Just think of all the lives you'll save if he heeds your warning. You'll be doing everyone a favor. Handy?" Fia motioned, and Handy carried over a chair. "Remember: 'There will be an attack at dawn.' Short and simple."

Gren sat down and closed her eyes. She didn't need to close them to wander, but sometimes it was easier. She started to search. She could tell there were hundreds of people sleeping, dreaming. She reached out farther, toward the clearing in the forest. She wasn't sure how she was supposed to pick out one person from all the dreams.

Suddenly, she remembered the sleep tonic. It sometimes left traces. If she could find that . . . .

There it was, like a light mist. She reached out, about to enter ...then pulled back.

Just how did this Vomat person end up taking the tonic?

Gren remembered what she and Lawson had discussed. Doing what Fia wanted could cost hundreds...maybe thousands...of lives. Fia had already resorted to kidnapping and threats to reach her own ends. Wandering wouldn't save anyone.

Gren took a deep breath as she wandered into a dream. "There will be an attack at dawn," she said softly, but out loud.

"Huh?" Lawson replied. It was his dream she'd wandered into.

"I'll explain later," she promised, this time not mouthing the words. She opened her eyes. "I delivered your message."

"Good girl," Fia replied. "Handy, have Lawson brought to the main dining area. Tell him we'll have a surprise for him soon."

"Whatever ya say, ma'am," Handy replied, heading toward the lift.

"What about me?" Gren asked.

"I thought we could just take a few more micros and enjoy this beautiful night," Fia responded. "This is the best weather I've seen in... Oh, look, Gren, a star!"

Gren looked up as a single star shone through a hole in the clouds. She was suddenly overcome with peace, as if she had done the right thing by not wandering Vomat's dream. She wouldn't be the cause of hundreds of deaths. She refused to become involved in a war that didn't concern her. She didn't know what the cost would be, but she knew she had at least bought some time. "It's beautiful," she said at last. "I wonder if the same star can be seen on Terra."

"Probably." Fia seemed lost, as if in a trance. "You did a wonderful thing tonight, Gren. If all goes according to plan, the war will be over soon. No more needless loss of life. Your action will bring the first peace that most Abacuans have ever known."

An uneasy feeling gnawed the pit of Gren's stomach. Maybe she hadn't done the right thing, after all.

Chapter Twenty-One

Roy ran to the cockpit, faster than he had moved in a long time. "What happened?"

"I'm . . . I'm not sure," Calli stammered. "I think we hit something."

Roy checked the readouts. "The odds of that happenin' are about a million to... Holy splarsh, ya're right!" Tayo gasped at Roy's use of the impolite expression. "Sorry, Tayo, it just kind of slipped out. No offense meant."

"What's going on?" Titus asked. "Is the damage bad?"

"Readouts are okay." Roy manually took over the controls and shut down the engines. He then set Puck to drift away from the planet. "We're fine for now. I'm worried about landin', though. I need to take a look outside. According to the readouts, fixin' her should be pretty easy. Sham, I want ya to come with me."

"Outside?" Sham asked. "You mean...in space?"

Roy nodded. "Yeah. I bet ya'll even like zero gravity."

Tayo and Calli were arguing again. It had started quietly but was growing louder by the micro. Each blamed the other for the accident.

"I'd like zero gravity," Titus remarked hopefully.

"No," Roy said quickly. "I need ya inside, to keep Puck steady. Plus we're gettin' close to Abacu. We need to stay out of the gravitational pull as long as possible."

"But they can..." Titus started, pointing at the girls.

"*No*," Roy repeated. "I'm not puttin' our lives in the hands of two people who can't get along for even a hundred."

Tayo glared at Roy, while Calli looked ashamed. Roy ran over a few things with Titus and then headed for the airlock, Sham close behind him.

The airlock was the one area of Puck that Sham had yet to see. They walked through a door into a small room. The door closed behind them. Roy pushed a couple of buttons and a cabinet opened, revealing a number of shiny silver outfits. "Pressure suits," Roy explained, starting to put one on. "They'll keep us safe. They have enough oxygen for a couple of units, which should be plenty of time."

"I don't know . . ."

"We'll be fine," Roy said with a grin. "We're driftin' away from Abacu, which has bought us some time. There are handgrips the whole way. Just keep holdin' on."

"If it's so easy, what do you need me for?"

"Ya *never* send only one person out, unless there's no alternative," Roy explained. He grabbed a pack from the cabinet. "The repair kit is in here."

Sham was surprised. "That's all we need for repairs?"

"I hope so, or else I'll be sayin' a lot worse than 'holy splarsh'. If we need to, we can get help from the planet, but I'd rather not."

"Why?"

"Think about it," Roy replied. "It looks like the government took your friends. Just think what they could do with four more Dream Wanderers, even if ya all are still students."

"Oh."

"Come on, Sham, get goin'," Roy urged the young Blue. "You're wastin' time."

Sham still held the pressure suit in his hand. "I don't know if I can do this."

Roy put a hand on Sham's shoulder. "I asked ya to be the one to come out with me because I trust ya. It'll be fine. Ya might even like it. As I said before, I bet ya'll like zero gravity. Have ya noticed the gravity has been changin' on the ship?" Sham shook his head as he started to put on the suit. "The gravity on Abacu is slightly stronger than on Terra. One of Puck's nice features is a built-in Gradual Artificial Gravity Changer. I can set the gravity to how it was where we left, and to what it will be at our destination. During the journey, it'll slowly increase or decrease. That makes it easier on us."

He helped Sham finish with the suit. Then he looped a wire cable with a fastener on the end around his own waist and handed another to Sham. "Ya ready?"

"I don't know . . ."

"Good." Roy pressed in another code, and the door in front of them opened. "Ya want to go first?"

"No," Sham said quickly, "I'll follow you."

An icy silence filled the cockpit. Calli and Tayo refused to look at each other. Titus sat in the pilot's chair, Calli the co-pilot's, and Tayo watched some readouts on the side.

"There!" Titus exclaimed. "They're out. We can follow their progress from here." He shook his head. "It's not fair! I wish I could be out there, too."

"Oh, and I supposed that's *my* fault," Tayo said.

"Of course it's your fault," Calli replied. "Everyone else trusts Roy. *We* know he's going to help us find Gren and Lawson. But you? No, all you've done is complain the entire time."

"We're basing this entire trip on a piece of torn cloth! We don't know that Gren and Lawson were kidnapped and taken to Abacu. For all we know, they *did* run away together. It's not like they ever tried to hide the fact that they have feelings for each other, and Lawson used to joke all the time about wandering on the Black Market."

"Come on, Tayo," Calli said. "Joking is one thing, actually doing it is another. And Gren would *never* agree to it. She has too much to lose."

"But Lawson has nothing," Tayo reminded her. "And Ladinda *was* threatening to break up their partnership. Maybe it was just too much for them to handle."

"If you were missing, wouldn't you want someone to look for you?"

"Yes," Tayo replied, "but I wouldn't want everyone basing their search on a torn piece of cloth. I would . . . I don't know . . . I'd want my friends to look for more clues before they took off across the galaxy."

"Would you two shut up?" Titus said. "If you keep acting like this, you'll be switching partners yet again...or worse, you'll be released from the program. Is that what you want?"

"I hate to break it to you, Titus," Tayo said, "but we're not going back to the Learning Center. If we survive this trip and actually return to Terra, and if our parents don't kill us for taking off without so much as a note, we'll be expelled as soon as we return to the Learning Center."

"Why do you think that?" Titus asked.

"Because Sham found evidence and didn't turn it in," Tayo reminded him. "At the very least we'll be expelled. There was a criminal investigation going on because of the missing sleep tonic. Who knows? We might all end up in the labor camps."

As Titus let Tayo's words sink in, the icy silence returned. "It looks like they're almost at the damaged spot," he observed at last.

"And it's *my* fault that something hit us as well, isn't it?" Tayo said.

"I never said that!" Calli shot back.

Titus turned up the earpiece for his communicator. If Roy needed to tell him something, he wanted to be sure to hear him above the constant bickering.

Roy had been right; the lack of gravity was unlike anything Sham had ever experienced. Slowly and carefully, he took hold of the handgrips and followed Roy. He wasn't sure why Roy had needed him there...he wasn't doing anything...but he was suddenly grateful for the opportunity. He had never felt so free.

It didn't take long to reach the damage. Roy attached the cable around his waist to one of the grips then took the pack off of his back. "Doesn't look too bad," he said.

Listening through the communicator was a strange. Roy's voice sounded hollow, distant. "What do you need me to do?" Sham asked.

"Nothin' yet," Roy replied. "Just come as close as ya can. Attach yourself the same way that I have, but keep holdin' on, as well. Extra safety never hurt anyone."

Sham did as he was told. As he moved closer, he caught his first glimpse of the area that had been hit. It was so small it almost didn't seem worth the effort. "That's it?"

"That," Roy said, "could cause us to burn up once we enter the atmosphere. But it's easy enough to fix...just need to fill the hole and patch it."

"It felt like something bigger hit us."

"I know what ya mean," Roy replied, filling the hole with some type of goo. "My guess is that Puck wasn't happy at bein' hit. She can be very temperamental."

"You talk about her as if she's alive."

Roy grinned, although the smile was invisible behind his facemask. "Are ya sayin' she's not?" He chuckled. "I know she's not alive, Sham, but sometimes a vehicle can take on a personality. And the reason it felt like a bigger hit was most likely an evasive action. My guess would be that there was more debris out there somewhere. When she's in automatic, she'll adjust for things like that."

"Oh."

Roy pulled a thin sheet of metal from the pack, placed it on top of the goo, and patted it down. "That should hold her. Looks good. Let's head back in."

They unattached the cables and reached for the next handgrip. Unhurriedly and meticulously they moved back toward the outside door to the airlock.

"We're almost there," Roy called, reaching for the next handgrip. Suddenly, the ship jerked. He missed the grip and started to float away.

Acting quickly, Sham attached the cable that was still around his waist to the closest handgrip. He then pushed off. The cable held, and he grabbed Roy around the ankle and pulled him back toward the ship.

Neither of them said a word until they were safely inside the airlock.

"Sayin' thanks doesn't seem like enough," Roy said.

"No problem," Sham replied with a grin. "You would have done the same thing for me. Now I see what you meant about not going out alone. I wonder what caused Puck to jerk like that."

"I can't say for sure," Roy said, removing the last part of his pressure suit, "but I wouldn't be surprised if it had somethin' to do with a couple of Greens who are havin' a hard time gettin' along."

Chapter Twenty-Two

Placing a hand on Lawson's shoulder, Handy guided the young Blue down the hall. Lawson asked endless questions about where they were going and why. Handy tried his best to ignore him. They stopped and Handy punched in a code, causing a door to open.

The room they entered had several tables and seating for a hundred people. The seats were empty and the tables were bare, except for one in the back. "What are we doing here?" Lawson asked.

"Will ya please just shut up?" Handy pleaded. "I swear, you're as bad as that girlfriend of yours."

"She's not my girlfriend," Lawson stated automatically. "But how is Gren? Is she all right?"

"Your girlfriend is fine," Handy answered, ignoring Lawson's declaration. "Just fine."

"What are we doing here?"

"Captain Fia told me to bring ya here. She said we'll have a surprise for ya real soon."

"A good surprise or a bad surprise?"

Handy just grinned. He sat down without answering the question, and started to whistle.

"Am I going to be able to see Lawson now?" Gren asked Captain Fia. They were back in the lift.

"Yes," Fia replied. "I've told you all along that when you do what we ask, you will be rewarded. Since you performed the task I requested, you'll be given a few hundreds with your partner."

"Only a few hundreds?" The disappointment showed in Gren's voice.

"You'll have a meal together."

They stepped out of the lift and walked down the hall. "A decent meal," she said, "in total privacy. No one will be watching or listening...you have my word."

Gren didn't think Captain Fia's word was worth much, but she decided to keep that thought to herself.

"I was proud of you tonight," Fia continued. "Your help in stopping this war . . ." She wiped a tear from her eye. "I know the circumstances haven't been fair to you and Lawson, but some rotation your names will be great here on Abacu. You, Gren, will be remembered as the one who brought peace."

"What's the war about, anyway?" Gren asked.

Fia sighed. "Fear. Oppression. Enslaving people to make them do what someone else wants."

"Like what you've done to Lawson and me?" Gren regretted the words immediately.

They stopped in front of a door. Fia looked directly at Gren. "Ironic, isn't it? As much as I appreciate your help, remember that I will do *anything* to make sure you keep helping us. There's a reason we brought you both here, Gren. Not only are you an extremely talented Wanderer, but you and Lawson have a strong connection. I will use that to my advantage in any way I must." She punched in a code and the door opened.

"Gren!" Lawson's shout of joy was probably heard throughout the entire building. He stood and ran to her. He wanted to throw his arms around her and never let go, but he stopped short. Out of respect for his partner and a growing respect for the Learning Center, he decided to obey their rules...no matter how stupid they still seemed.

"Are you okay?" Gren asked.

"Yes, Lawson, how are you?" Captain Fia wanted to know. "I haven't seen you since we arrived. Is everyone treating you fairly?"

"It depends on how you define 'fairly'."

"You still have your fighting spirit," Fia remarked. "It's a good thing for both of you that Gren has decided to cooperate. Come on, Handy, let's leave these two alone. I promised them total privacy."

"We'll see ya in a unit or so," Handy said.

"Enjoy your meal," Fia added.

No one said another word until the door had closed. "We're actually alone," Lawson said. "Do you really think we have total privacy?"

"No," Gren whispered quickly. "Captain Fia made a point of insisting to me that no one would be listening. Makes me thinks they probably are."

"Makes sense." Lawson pointed to the table in the back. "Looks like they've got something set up for us." They walked in that direction.

Gren chuckled. "I was surprised you didn't try to hug me when I first came in."

Lawson looked down, embarrassed. "I've been doing a lot of thinking. The Learning Center has its rules. They're in place for a reason. We may not know why, but I'm sure Ladinda does. Besides you, I have nothing but the Learning Center and the future it promises. It's about time I start taking it a little more seriously."

"Hutch would be proud to hear you say that."

Lawson laughed. "More like shocked."

They sat down and started to eat. "Have they been treating

you okay?" Lawson asked.

"I'm fine." Gren paused. "I was on the roof of the building with Captain Fia tonight."

"In the rain?"

"No," Gren said. "It wasn't raining. We even saw a star. Stars must not be all that common. Fia was really moved by it."

"I wonder why. On the way here all we could see were stars."

"Yeah, but I think it's rare for the planet." Gren chose her words carefully. She was sure someone was listening and didn't want anyone to know into whose dream she had really delivered the message. "She asked me to deliver a message into the dream of Vomat, the commander of that camp she showed us when we first arrived here."

Lawson knew exactly what she was trying to say. "Oh. What was the message?"

"There will be an attack at dawn."

"Wow," Lawson replied. "Scary-sounding message."

"Yeah, I know," Gren agreed. "But what do I care about these people or the ones on Eden? Their war doesn't concern me. All I care about, Lawson, is making sure you're safe. So if they need me to deliver their stupid message, I will." Gren almost hoped someone was listening. "I just wish we could go home."

"Yeah," Lawson agreed. "We'll need to figure out what we're going to tell them back at the Learning Center. No one will *ever* believe this. I'd hate to be expelled for something that's not out fault."

"We'll think of something." Gren was glad to hear Lawson speak positively about their schooling. It seemed a long time ago that he had spoken of running away.

As they ate their meal they continued to converse, grateful for each other's company. Both were careful about what they said; they knew they could discuss strategy in each other's dreams. They were both certain that someone was listening to their conversation.

· ◦ ◖◗◖ ◦ ·

In a room down the hall, Handy paced. "It's not fair, Captain. It's the first time in rotations that they're together. Wouldn't ya love to know what they're sayin'?"

"Handy," Fia said, an authoritative tone in her voice, "I gave them my word. I promised them total privacy, and that's what they're going to have. Understand?"

"Whatever ya say, ma'am."

Chapter Twenty-Three

Neither Calli nor Tayo would admit that she might have done anything to make the ship jerk, but it was obvious even more was wrong between them. They had stopped speaking to each other, their words replaced by quick glances or glaring stares. Although no one voiced it, all four students feared that Roy's patch wouldn't hold.

It did. Entering the atmosphere was no problem.

"The hard part," Roy explained, "will be findin' the best place to land." As they approached, they could see Royal City. Roy purposely steered away. "The forest will be better."

"How about over there?" Sham asked, pointing to a large clearing.

Roy shook his head. "Not a good idea. Chances are that's where Eden's Attack Force is stationed. Don't know much about who they are or what they're like lately. We need to keep as low a profile as possible."

"So what are we looking for?" Titus asked.

"A place big enough to land, but small enough that we can hide Puck, so she won't be visible from above."

"How about over there?" Calli asked, indicating a small spot in the distance.

"I think you're right, Calli," Roy said with a grin. "That looks perfect."

Calli beamed as Tayo continued to glower at her partner.

After a safe landing, the four students took turns changing out of their uniforms in the necessary room, while Roy packed some bags. He mumbled to himself as he worked, going over a list in his mind.

Tayo was the first one ready. "Ya look good," he told her as he stuffed some rations into one of the packs.

"I look stupid." Tayo looked down at herself. "I haven't worn anything besides my uniform since I entered the program. And these clothes don't fit. They're way too big."

"Ya're right," Roy replied, controlling the anger in his voice. "They looked a whole lot better on my wife."

Tayo felt terrible. "Roy, I didn't mean..."

"Listen, Tayo," Roy interrupted, "I know ya don't like me and ya know what? I don't really care. I'm doin' this because your friends are in trouble and ya didn't know any other way to help them. I'm gettin' nothin' out of this...nothin' at all. I'm here because Sham asked me for help, and he's an old friend. And remember...I didn't force ya to come along. So drop the attitude or stay behind."

"I just . . ." Tayo decided not to finish her sentence. "Do you need any help?"

Roy chuckled. "Yeah, that would be good. Help me double-check, make sure we got everythin'."

Tayo stared at the packs in front of her. "How much stuff do we need?"

"I doubt we'll be comin' back here until after we've rescued your friends. So, unless you're a skilled hunter . . ."

"No." Tayo shivered.

Roy nodded. "That's what I thought. Could ya grab that pair of magnifiers for me off the top shelf?"

"These?" Tayo took them down and handed them to Roy. "Here you go."

"Thanks," Roy said, stuffing them into one of the packs.

Calli, who had just changed out of her uniform, listened from the back. "Looks who's finally getting along," she mumbled to herself.

"Hey, Calli," Roy said, "I need a favor. In the cockpit, under the pilot's seat, there's a box. Could ya bring it to me please?"

"Sure, Roy," Calli said sweetly. She returned a few hundreds later. "This?"

"Yeah, thanks." Roy took the box from her. "I have a map in here, somewhere." He rifled through the box, then stopped. He sat down, holding something in his hand. Whatever it was had obviously thrown him. "I forgot this was in here," he said, more to himself than to the girls.

"Is it the map?" Calli asked quietly, knowing that it wasn't.

"Nah, it's Breeze and me." Roy wiped a tear from the corner of his eye. "The rotation we were joined." He stared at the picture for several more hundreds. "Wanna see it?" he asked at last.

Her hand shaking, Calli took the picture. Roy was unmistakable, although he was quite a bit younger. He wore an army uniform. The woman next to him was dressed in white, her face barely visible through a veil. "You look happy," Calli commented, handing the picture to Tayo.

"Happiest rotation of my life," Roy replied. He wiped away another tear, then smiled. Calli and Tayo stood next to each other. "If I'd known that somethin' as simple as a picture would make the two of ya get along, I'd have brought a whole lot more. If ya start actin' like ya actually *like* each other, who knows? We might survive this trip after all."

"Why wouldn't we survive?" Tayo asked nervously.

Roy laughed and started once again to look for the map.

When the boys were finally ready, everyone stepped out of

Puck. A light rain was falling. Roy set the security system, and the five of them walked away. Each had a pack on his or her back. "The gravity is a little stronger here than what you're used to," Roy explained, "but Puck has helped compensate for that. If ya get tired, let me know. The packs might slow us down a bit, but we don't have anythin' that we don't need."

"Where are we headed?" Sham asked.

"When we flew over Royal City, did ya notice that one purplish building towering over the rest of them?" The four students all nodded. "Unless things have changed since the last time I was here, that's the army's headquarters. That's probably where they have your friends."

"What if they're not there?" Tayo asked skeptically.

"Then I guess we'll have to find out just how good ya are at wanderin' dreams."

"We're not allowed to wander someone's dream without permission," Titus reminded him.

Roy sighed. "At the very least, one of ya will have to try to wander either Gren or Lawson's dream. It will probably be the only way to make contact. Don't ya think they'd want to know we're here, that we want to get them back home?"

"Yeah," Titus said.

"Then there's your permission. I'm not askin' ya to do anythin' immoral, Titus. Just to help your friends." Roy looked at the map. "This way."

They hiked for several units, taking food or water breaks from time to time. They continued until well after dark. Finally, they stopped. Roy gave Sham and Titus instructions for setting up the two tents, while he had the girls follow him. They continued through the dark woods with only a small light to see by. They hiked for almost half a unit. "There," Roy whispered, pointing in the distance. "That's the army's headquarters."

"That big building, way far away?" Calli asked.

Roy nodded. "Hand me the magnifiers." Tayo took them out of the bag she still carried and gave them to him. Roy stared into them, adjusting them as necessary. Then he handed them back to Tayo. "Look on the roof, tell me what ya see."

Tayo thought Roy was insane. The building was barely visible from where they were...how could she tell what was on the roof? She looked through the magnifiers and was instantly surprised at how well they worked. On the corner of the roof she could see the profiles of two people. One was a woman and the other . . .

"Holy splarsh, that's Gren!"

"That's what I thought," Roy said.

"Is Lawson there?" Calli asked.

"No." Without being asked, Tayo handed the magnifiers to her partner.

Calli anxiously gazed through them. "Who is that with her?"

Roy took the magnifiers back and looked again. "I'm not a hundred percent sure, but I think that's Fia. She's wearin' captain's insignia. Doesn't surprise me...she was young, but movin' up pretty fast through the ranks when I was there. If I remember correctly, she's from Terra, a former Dream Wanderin' student herself who got kicked out of the program. She's one dangerous woman. They're lookin' out toward Eden's camp. Wait a micro, someone has joined them. A man. No. It can't be..." Roy handed the magnifiers back to Calli.

"Who is he?" Calli asked.

"They call him Handy," Roy replied. "He's my cousin."

Chapter Twenty-Four

Feeling a lot less nervous than the first time, Gren returned to the roof with Captain Fia. She and Lawson had discussed the situation in their dreams; Gren planned to try what she had done before. She knew it was only a matter of time until she got caught, but what would Fia do? She wouldn't kill Lawson; he was what Fia held over Gren's head. Gren was worried that Lawson could be tortured, but it had eventually dawned on them that, so far, no one had hurt either of them. It was looking more and more like Captain Fia was all threats, no action.

"Sorry, Gren, it's not as nice out tonight," Fia commented. The two of them were alone. Fia held the communicator Handy had used last time. A steady, cold drizzle was falling. "This shouldn't take long." She glanced around. "I was hoping someone might have left some chairs covered up, but it doesn't look like we're that lucky."

"That's okay," Gren replied. "I can wander standing."

Fia smiled. "No arguments this time?"

"Why bother?" Gren replied, a fake defeatist tone in her voice. "The sooner we get this over with, the sooner we can return home, right? Besides, I'd like to see Lawson again."

"I never said that you'd get to see him for wandering this time," Fia said, "but if that's what it takes to avoid the arguing, I'll think about it for next time."

"Please, let me see him."

Fiddling with the communicator, Fia ignored Gren's cry. "That long ago?" she said. "Then we don't have much time. Don't worry. We're ready on this end." She turned her attention back toward Gren. "Same man as last time."

"Vomat?"

"Right. He didn't listen to his dream before, but we expected that. A few dreams coming true should change his mind."

"What's the message?" Gren wanted to know.

"It's slightly longer," Fia told her. "Tell Vomat, 'You didn't listen last time, and a lot of good warriors died. The next attack will be from the east, around the time of the mid-rotation meal.' Got it?"

"'You didn't listen last time, and a lot' . . . what was it again?"

Fia hoped Gren wasn't stalling for time. "'You didn't listen last time, and a lot of good warriors died. The next attack will be from the east, around the time of the mid-rotation meal.' Will I have to write these down for you from now on?"

"No," Gren said. "I think I have it. 'You didn't listen last time, and a lot of good warriors died. The next attack will be from the east, around the time of the mid-rotation meal.' Anything else?"

"Not now," Fia replied. "But we're in a hurry because he already took the tonic, so you'd better get started."

Gren closed her eyes and, ignoring Fia's warning, took her time. She wasn't really stalling; she just wanted to make it look like she was searching for one specific, sleeping individual far away. To make sure the assignment wasn't a trap, she found Vomat's dream, but she didn't quite enter, just hit the edge. Then she reached out for Lawson. "'You didn't listen last time, and a lot of good warriors died. The next attack will be from the east, around the time of the mid-rotation meal.'" She mouthed the words as she wandered.

She opened her eyes again. "Done."

"Mouthing the words, nice touch," Fia remarked. "I take it that was for my benefit?"

"Partially," Gren replied. "It was also easier for me to remember, to make sure I delivered the whole message. That was a long one."

"Another job well done," Fia said. "Are you ready to..." She jumped as Handy touched her shoulder. "Don't go sneaking up on me like that!"

"Sorry, Captain," Handy replied. "I just thought ya might want to know . . ." He whispered something in her ear.

"Well, you know what to do!" she said. "Now!"

"Whatever ya say, ma'am," Handy replied. He glanced out into the dark for a micro.

"Handy, I said *now*."

"Sorry, Captain," Handy said. "It's just that I thought I saw somethin'."

"What?" Fia asked.

"I'm not sure." Handy turned. "I'll go take care of that other little problem."

"Thank you, Handy."

"What's happening?" Gren asked, watching Handy disappear into the darkness on the roof. She was shivering; she wished the rain would stop.

"None of your business," Fia replied coldly. She took a deep breath, then smiled. "I'm sorry, that was rude. You came up here with me tonight without one complaint, at least not a big one. You're standing here, getting all wet . . . How about a nice, hot bath and some clean clothes? That would be a good reward, wouldn't it?"

"I'd rather see Lawson."

"Looking the way you do? Gren, you're a beautiful girl, but

right now... Well, I'd have thought *no* woman would want her boyfriend to see her the way you look right now."

"Lawson's not my boyfriend."

"Whatever you say," Fia said with a wink. "But you can't see Lawson right now; we might need him for something else." Her grin spread across her face. "Although maybe, he might have a chance to earn the right to see you, instead of the other way around. That is, if Handy's hunch is right."

"How?" Gren asked.

Fia ignored the question. "Come on, let's get you inside and cleaned up. For your reward, you get to take a bubble bath in my personal suite. I have some wonderful scented bath gel; it's absolutely marvelous. You'll love it." She started walking forward. "Admit it, a hot bath sounds pretty good right."

Gren walked beside her. "That might be nice."

Fia laughed. "Might be nice? That's an understatement if ever I heard one!"

It was more than Gren had expected. Fia had taken her into her private quarters, which were even more luxurious than those of the ship that had brought them there. The bathing area in the necessary room was huge. The warm water and bubbles were relaxing. Soft music played in the background. Gren closed her eyes for a micro, allowing herself to escape for just a hundred or so.

"Whoa, Gren, I was expecting you to be wandering me," a voice said. "But when that didn't happen, I thought I'd give it a shot. Where are you?"

Gren glanced around, terrified. She was at a camp of some type, in the middle of a battle. She took a few steps forward; someone fell dead at her feet. In the distance, she saw a man and knew it was Vomat. She was trying to reach him, to deliver him a message, but no matter how hard she tried she couldn't catch up. "Lawson? Is that you? You'd better get out of here... there's a war going on!"

"You're dreaming, Gren," Lawson said calmly. "This isn't really happening. The only part that's real is that I'm wandering your dream. The rest of it is from the message you were supposed to deliver to Vomat, but you gave it to me instead. Remember?"

On the left, Gren could see a long table filled with untouched food. She tried to think as explosions occurred all around her. "You didn't listen last time, and a lot of good warriors died. The next attack will be from the east, around the time of the mid-rotation meal," she mumbled. "Lawson, did it come true? Are people dying because I didn't deliver the message?"

"No," Lawson said firmly. "This is just your imagination, your fear that something bad is going to happen because you didn't do as you were told. But remember, Gren, Fia is using you, using *us*. They have some kind of plan that *will* cause the deaths of thousands of people if you listen to her. That's why she told you that you'll be the one to end the war. Remember?"

Gren nodded.

"Now," Lawson said, "I want you to turn around. There's no battle going on behind you. See?" Gren did as she was told. "Walk forward and keep going. You'll soon see a lake, just like the one at the Learning Center. It's right up ahead. See it?"

"Lawson, I see it!"

"Run to it, Gren. Once you sit on the beach, the battle will be over and you won't be able to hear anything or anyone but me."

"What about birds?"

"Okay," Lawson conceded, "I know how much you love

birds. Maybe you'll hear one or two in the distance."

Gren reached the beach and sat down. She smiled and pointed up to the sky. "There, Lawson! There's one now!"

Lawson laughed. "Good job. Now, Gren, forget about the birds. I need you to concentrate on what happened tonight Captain Fia obviously had another message. Did anything else happen?"

Gren, noticing that she wore her uniform, crossed her arms in front of her. "I got to take a bath. In fact . . . never mind."

Hoping that Gren couldn't hear it, Lawson suppressed another chuckle. "That's it? She gave you the message, and you got to take a bath?"

Gren squinted, trying to remember something. "Handy showed up while we were on the roof. He whispered something to Fia. She told him to take care of it, and then he left. Fia looked kind of worried, but she wouldn't tell me what was going on. Then she said something about you."

"Me?"

"Yeah." Gren hated trying to remember facts in dreams; things tended to jumble together. "She said *you* might have the chance to earn the right to see *me*, instead of the other way around. She said something about Handy's hunch, but she wouldn't give me a clue as to what she was talking about. I guess there's going to be someone for you to wander, too."

"Why would they want me to wander?" Lawson asked, more to himself than to Gren. "You're better at it then I am, and they know that."

"It seemed kind of spur of the moment," Gren remembered. "Like she'd just come up with an idea. Maybe it has nothing to do with wandering at all. Maybe it's something else."

"Something else?" Lawson repeated. "I wonder what."

"Wonder or wander?" Gren started to laugh.

"That joke is getting so old," Lawson replied. He didn't have much time; he could tell that Gren was waking up. "I'll talk to you again soon."

He left Gren's dream, worried about Fia's plans for him.

Chapter Twenty-Five

"Your cousin?" Tayo repeated, grabbing the magnifiers from Calli and looking through them. "You still know people on Abacu?"

"What, I'm not allowed to have family?" Roy sounded slightly irritated.

Calli shook her head. "I'm sure that's not what my partner meant. She thought...we both thought...that you cut all ties when you moved to Terra, that's all."

"Blood's not a tie ya can easily cut," Roy said. He took back the magnifiers. "I haven't seen him, or anyone else from Abacu for that matter, in orbits." He looked through the magnifiers again. "Well, Handy's leavin'. Looks like he's in a bit of a hurry. Your friend seems cold."

"I can't imagine why," Tayo said with a shiver. She hated the cold rain.

Roy watched for a little while longer. "They're goin' in now, too." He put the magnifiers down. "I guess that means we can head back, let the boys know that at least Gren is here. We'll get a good night's sleep, then work on the rescue plan at dawn." He looked directly at Tayo. "Unless ya have any other ideas."

"No," she replied, embarrassed.

"Do you think Sham was able to get a fire started?" Calli asked as they started to walk.

"Sham, do anything useful?" Tayo said. "You have got to be kidding me."

"What's your problem with Sham?" Calli said. "He and I have been friends for . . . for . . . for longer than you and I will ever be!"

"That's fine with me," Tayo shot back. "But at least *I'd* be able to make a fire, even with all this wet wood."

"Would ya please give it a rest?" Roy pleaded. "And Sham better not have made a fire. The smoke would be visible from the top of the headquarters. We don't need the entire army findin' out we're here."

The march back to the camp seemed to take forever. Although they walked mostly in silence, from time to time anger burst out between Tayo and Calli. Tayo accused Calli of snapping a branch in her face; Calli was sure that Tayo purposely didn't tell her about a rock in her path.

Roy looked forward to the longer periods of silence, although the air was filled with resentment. How these two had been partnered he didn't understand.

"Eww, what did you just throw on me?" Tayo almost screamed, trying to wipe a wet leaf off her face.

"I didn't throw anything," Calli yelled back. "If you think I'd stoop to your level..."

"Would the two of ya just stop!" Roy's voice was filled with anger, but he kept his volume down. "If we're goin' to rescue your friends, we're goin' to have to work together as a team. This constant bickerin' won't help them. Are the two of ya goin' to work together, or do I take Sham and Titus with me and just leave ya here?"

"You wouldn't," Tayo challenged.

Roy sighed. "No, I wouldn't. But believe me, the two of ya are makin' me think about it. So if ya can't get along, just shut up."

They traveled the next few hundreds in relative silence. Soon, they came upon the campsite. The tents were set up, the packs stored inside. Neither Titus nor Sham was anywhere to be seen. "They couldn't have gone far," Calli observed. She put her hands around her mouth, ready to call. "Sha..."

"No," Roy said quickly. "We can't call attention to ourselves." He walked around the perimeter of the campsite, obviously looking for something.

"'Call attention to ourselves," Tayo repeated. "What are you talking about?"

"And what are you looking for?" Calli asked.

"Here," Roy said, pointing. "This is where they started their precious fire. I should have realized they might and told them . . . and over here. Ya see how the leaves look trampled, some of the branches broken down? Sham and Titus weren't the only ones here. Looks like they put up a fight."

"So where are they?" Calli asked, worried.

"This is only a guess," Roy started, "but they're probably with Gren and Lawson. Or they will be soon. Looks like we're on our own, ladies."

"They've been captured?" Calli's voice quavered. "The army won't hurt the boys, will they?"

Roy shrugged. "Ya saw Gren, she didn't appear to be injured. As long as they do as they're told, they'll be fine. The army doesn't have a reputation for harmin' children. Hopefully Titus and Sham will make something' up, a way that they got here that doesn't include all of us. We better get movin', though. Someone might be back. We can take a few things with us, but we want the camp to look untouched." He stuffed some food and some other items into a bag. "Come on, time to get goin'." Roy hurried away, with Calli and Tayo close behind.

For close to a unit, they walked in almost complete silence. "Here, this will do," Roy said at last. The trees were thicker where he stopped. Some low bushes partially blocked the steady drizzle. "I want the two of ya to crawl under there. At least it's a bit drier. There's a lightweight blanket in the bag. Try to get some sleep... you're goin' to need your strength."

"Where are you going to be?" Calli asked, her voice still shaking.

"I'm goin' back to the campsite, see if there's somethin' I missed," Roy replied. "Maybe I was bein' an alarmist before. Maybe they just went to look for drier wood."

"Do you really think that?" Tayo asked.

Roy shook his head. "No. I'll be back in a couple of units."

The two girls wrapped themselves up together in the lone blanket. It was thin, but it was also provided a lot of warmth. Although they were both soaked to the skin, the blanket was somehow comforting.

"I'm sorry," Tayo said at last. "I know I've been rather . . . difficult the past couple of rotations."

"Difficult?" Calli raised her voice more than she had intended. "You've done nothing but . . ." She paused, realizing it was pointless to fight. "I'm sorry, too. We have to start working together. What do you think we should do?"

Tayo paused. "Well, as Roy said, we should probably try to get some sleep. And who knows, maybe we'll get lucky, and Sham or Titus will try to wander, let us know what happened."

"Sleep. I feel like we should be doing something more."

"I know it's kind of a lame plan," Tayo admitted, "but it's the only one we have."

"It's not lame," Calli said, lying down and trying to make herself comfortable. "I just hope that either Sham or Titus is up to the task."

Chapter Twenty-Six

Alone at a table in a small, dark room, Lawson sat for what felt like an eternity. He was worried what Captain Fia might ask him to do...or do to him. It probably had something to do with wandering, but that didn't make sense. Gren was a much better wanderer than he could ever hope to be. She had developed an impression of range and direction that he would never understand, and she was patient. He did well for his orbit because he pushed himself, trying to keep up with his partner.

Lawson was growing more confused by the micro. He tried to reach out to Gren, but she wasn't dreaming. He drummed his fingers on the table and waited.

After a few hundreds that felt like units, Fia entered. Lawson took a deep breath, reminding himself that if he didn't screw things up, he might be allowed to see Gren. He also made a mental note that he wasn't supposed to know that information.

"Lawson," Fia said with artificial sweetness, "I trust you're being treated well."

"As well as . . ." Lawson decided not to argue. "I'm fine," he mumbled. "How's Gren?"

Fia grinned. "You're both so predictable. I knew you'd ask about her immediately. She's doing very well. In fact, since she completed a little task for me earlier, she was allowed some time to pamper herself. She does miss you, though. Would you like to see her?"

Lawson sat up straighter. "Yes, please."

"Oh, you're so polite. It's no surprise she's crazy about you. You can see her soon...if you do me a little favor."

"What?" Lawson slumped back into his chair.

Captain Fia sat down across from him. "I just want to talk. A friendly little chat."

Lawson shook his head. "A friendly little chat about what?" Whatever information Fia wanted, he knew must be important if it could earn him a visit with Gren.

"The Learning Center," Fia replied. "As you know, I used to attend. I didn't make it as far as you have, but I have some very fond memories of the place. I told you before that I was partnered with Hutch, right?" Lawson nodded. "Did he ever mention me? Surely he must have mentioned he was partnered with a female, especially considering that you and Gren are about to achieve something once thought impossible."

"Nope." Lawson shook his head. "I don't remember him ever mentioning any partner."

Fia looked disappointed. "Oh. That's okay. How about Ladinda? Is she still strict?"

"She's strict but fair," Lawson replied, "most of the time. She talked about breaking up Gren and me for reasons that weren't our fault..."

Fia laughed. "Yes, I remember that rule. That's one rule they've always had but will never explain. So, besides Gren, who are your other friends? How about roommates? If things are still the same, you'd be in the same room as partnered Blues, correct?"

Lawson nodded. "Yeah, I have two roommates. Gren's situation is a little different. She's in with partnered Blues, but there are also partnered Greens in her room. These two girls haven't been able to keep partners, so Ladinda decided that, if she put them with girls an orbit ahead, then maybe..."

Fia cut him off. "Tell me about *your* roommates. What are

their names?"

It seemed a strange, yet harmless question. "Sham and Titus. Why?"

"What are they like?"

"They're kind of opposites," Lawson told her. "Sham likes to fool around; you can never tell if he's serious or not. Titus is usually fairly somber, but he opens up from time to time."

"What do they look like?"

Lawson thought for a micro; he wasn't used to describing his friends. "I don't know. Sham is kind of tall and skinny, with messy brown hair. Titus is shorter than I am, with black hair. Why?" he asked again.

Fia continued to ignore the question. "How close are the three of you?"

"Pretty close. I was supposed to spend the break with Sham. I usually spend it with Gren and her family, but Ladinda forbade it this time, for some stupid reason."

"Why not with you own family?"

Lawson looked down. "I don't have one. My parents died a long time ago."

"I'm sorry. I didn't know," Fia seemed sincere.

Lawson looked back up. "Do I get to see Gren now?"

"Maybe soon. So you were supposed to spend the break with, um, Sham? Was that his name?"

"Yeah." Lawson almost grinned. "It would have been great. His parents were going on vacation, so it would have been just the two of us."

"What did you have planned?"

"Not all that much," Lawson replied. "But it would have been nice...almost like we were out on our own."

"You had no plans at all?"

"Well," Lawson said, slightly embarrassed, "he was going to take me to meet an old friend of his. Sham hadn't seen him in orbits because his parents don't like him. Sham said he's crazy, but in a harmless sort of way."

Fia grew more interested. "Why does Sham think he's crazy?"

Lawson laughed. "You're not going to believe this, but this guy thinks he's from Abacu. Of course, that doesn't sound quite so crazy now. Maybe he really is."

"Of course he's crazy," Fia said, chuckling. "Did you ever see other ships like mine in the sky? No, my friend, he couldn't be from Abacu. So, does this madman have a name?"

Lawson thought for a micro. "I think it's Roy," he said at last.

Fia stopped laughing and stood up. "Lawson," she said as she entered her code into the keypad, "you've just earned yourself a visit with Gren. Follow me."

A few hundreds later, Lawson sat alone at another table, the conversation running through his mind. Why had Fia been so interested in his life at the Learning Center? The door opened, and Fia walked in, Gren at her side. "Your partner did good work, Gren," Fia said. "He was open and honest, not trying to fool me, lie to me, or annoy me in general. He's earned the two of you one unit, unsupervised. Have a nice chat!"

Gren sat at the table next to Lawson and placed her hand next to his. The desire to touch him, to let him hold her and ease her fears, was overwhelming, but she didn't give in. "What did you have to do?"

Although he was sure they weren't unsupervised as promised, Lawson decided to speak fairly freely. Of course, they would be expected to talk about what had happened since their last visit. "Captain Fia and I just talked," Lawson explained. "I have no idea how that earned us a unit, but I'm not complaining."

"What did you talk about?"

"Mostly the Learning Center," Lawson replied. "She asked about Hutch and Ladinda, and then we talked a little bit about my roommates."

"Sham and Titus? Why?"

"I have no idea." Lawson grinned. "I never really thought they were all that interesting. So, what have you been up to?"

"I had to wander again tonight. Same thing as last time. It was cold and rainy," Gren looked away, slightly embarrassed, "so Fia let me take a bath in her private quarters. I have to admit, it was nice."

Down the hall, Handy approached Fia. "Where do ya want me to put our new find?"

Fia tapped her fingers on her arm, thinking. "In with Lawson would probably be best. And make it fast. His unit with Gren will be over soon, and I think it would be a very nice surprise for him."

"Whatever ya say, ma'am."

When Gren's and Lawson's time together was over, Captain Fia took Gren back to her cell, while Lawson went with Handy. Lawson complained the whole way; he was sure they hadn't been allowed an entire unit. Handy ignored him, as usual, until they reached the door.

"Enough already," he said at last. "Now, if ya'll be a good boy and actually be quiet for a micro or two, I'll open the door. We've got a big surprise in there for ya."

"What kind of surprise?"

"That's not bein' quiet," Handy answered. He purposely

delayed several more micros. "Okay, since you're *finally* bein' quiet like a good boy, are ya ready?"

Lawson nodded, not saying a word. The only surprise he really wanted was a ride back to Terra with Gren, but he was curious.

"Good." Handy keyed in his code, and the door opened. Sitting on Lawson's bed, looking extremely disheveled, were Titus and Sham.

Chapter Twenty-Seven

Lawson stood still for several micros, trying to process what was going on. Why were his two roommates there with him, halfway across the galaxy? He tried to speak, but he couldn't figure out what to say.

Suddenly, it made some sense. Someone had captured the two Blues, and Captain Fia had grilled Lawson, trying to find out if they were telling the truth. "It's my bed...you're going to have to sleep on the floor," were the only words that came out of his mouth.

"Nice to see you, too," Sham replied sarcastically. "Aren't you just a little bit curious about why we're here?"

Lawson glanced up at what he thought was probably a camera, hoping that they understood not to say too much. "Okay, fine. Why are you here?"

"We came to rescue you," Titus replied.

"You've done a really great job of it." Lawson sat down on the edge of the bed, causing his roommates to move over. "So what happened? How did you know I was gone?"

"We heard you stormed out of your last wandering session," Sham explained. "We thought you'd just gone somewhere to calm down. But then the next morning, Gren asked us to help look for you. I found this." He pulled the piece of torn cloth out of his pocket.

"Roy told us it was from the Royal Abacuan Army," Titus added. Lawson shot him a worried glance.

"And so we borrowed Roy's ship and came here, looking for you," Sham continued, purposely leaving out several details.

"The System Workers have been looking for you and Gren," Titus told Lawson. "Some sleep tonic is missing. They think the two of you stole it and ran away. So what really happened? And where's Gren?"

Lawson sighed. "Gren's here too. She's fine. We were brought here so Gren could do some wandering. There's a war or something going on, and she's supposed to help them stop it."

"How?" Titus asked.

"They always warned us about the power of wandering," Lawson said. "Now I know why."

"It figures," Sham said. "No matter where we are, Ladinda can always find a way to teach us a lesson."

"This has nothing to do with Ladinda," Lawson told him. "There are two people Gren and I have been dealing with: Captain Fia and Handy."

"I think we met them both," Sham said, rubbing the back of his head. "Handy first, but then some woman asked us a whole lot of questions."

"As long as we've done what they told us to do, they've treated us fairly well." Lawson pulled up his feet, kicking Sham. "I'm going to sleep. As I said before, the bed is mine. But you can share the blanket; the floor is probably cold."

"Going to sleep?" Titus repeated, standing up. "How can you sleep with all this going on?"

"Believe me, my friend, there's not really all that much happening. A lot of sitting around with nothing to do but let your mind wander." Lawson hit the switch that turned out the lights, hoping they'd taken the hint.

Looking out the window of his dorm room, Lawson couldn't help but smile. It felt good to be back, even though he knew it wasn't real. How much longer would it take? When would it finally be over so they could return home? What would they tell Ladinda? He pushed those and other questions out of his mind and decided to enjoy the view.

"It's about time." Gren's voice was more playful than critical.

"Yeah, well, I was busy." Lawson paused to see if either of his roommates had realized what he was up to, but he couldn't sense their presence.

"Busy doing what?" Gren asked. "And what are we doing in your room? You know I'm not allowed in here."

"Hey, it's what's been on my mind. I can't always control what happens...my mind just sort of wanders. And I've been busy, explaining to Sham and Titus what's going on."

"Sham and Titus?" Gren paused and searched herself. "Where are they? I don't sense them in your dream."

"They're not, the idiots," Lawson replied. "I tried to hint to them. Anyway, I figure that's why Fia was asking me about them, to make sure they were telling her the truth."

"They're probably who Handy saw from the roof earlier. His hunch must have been that someone had come to save us. So where are they now?" Gren asked.

"Right here with me. They said they borrowed some ship to come here and rescue us, but I got the feeling that they weren't telling me everything. Wait a micro...Sham said it was Roy's ship."

"Who's Roy?"

"Sham's friend who claims he's from Abacu," Lawson explained. "Captain Fia was really interested before when I mentioned Roy...I think that's what earned me the visit with you. My guess is that someone else is here with them."

"I don't understand why they don't just try to wander you," Gren said.

"I'm pretty sure Sham is asleep," Lawson said. "If I slip back a little, I can hear him snoring. But I don't want to concentrate on it, because I don't want to break the connection with you."

"Sham is asleep? Lawson, let's see if he's dreaming. If he's not, I'll meet you back here in few hundreds. Only try to pick a different location. I don't feel comfortable in your room."

Pressure suit on, Sham took one last look around. He could see Calli and Tayo in the front, fighting over Puck's controls. Titus stood close by, a jealous look on his face. Roy had one hand on the airlock door. "Hurry up, will ya?" he was saying. "If we don't get this fixed, we're all goin' to die."

"There's no problem," Titus's voice said. "Puck doesn't need to be fixed. There's nothing wrong at all. Now come back here and take off that pressure suit. We need to talk."

"Titus?"

"Gren!" Titus's voice exclaimed. "Are you okay? How have they been treating you?"

"We're fine," Gren's voice replied. "Lawson, are you here yet?"

"Yeah," his voice answered. "It took me a second to shake off the other dream. Titus, Sham, you were supposed to follow me!"

"How were we supposed to know?" Titus's voice asked. "You weren't exactly giving us a whole lot of information."

"There's a camera in the room. We're being monitored," Lawson's voice explained. "Wandering has been the only way that Gren and I can talk."

"He's perfected the art of letting his mind wander," Gren's voice added.

"I thought he did that back when we were Whites," Titus's voice joked.

"Wait a micro," Sham said, looking around. "This is just too weird for me. What's going on?"

"Sham, my friend, you're being wandered," Lawson's voice explained. "By all three of us."

"You're not supposed to call him by name when you're wandering," Titus's voice reminded them.

"Hutch is wrong about that," Gren's voice said. "Maybe you shouldn't during a professional session, but Lawson and I have had no problem using each other's names."

"It actually helps," Lawson's voice agreed. "Puts us more at ease. So Titus, tell us what's really going on."

"We came to rescue you," Titus's voice explained.

"You've done a really great job of it," Gren's voice said sarcastically.

Lawson's voice laughed. "That's exactly what I said!"

"We came with Sham's friend Roy," Titus's voice continued. "He's originally from Abacu, and he flew us here. He went to get a better view of the big purple building, and then a group of men grabbed us."

"Where's Roy now?" Gren's voice asked.

"I don't know," Titus's voice answered. "We didn't tell anyone about him, just said we took his ship, but I don't think they believed us."

Sham kept looking around, trying to follow all of the voices inside his head. "So are you the only three who are going to show up, or should I expect two more?"

"Two more?" Lawson's voice repeated. "Why would anyone else show up? Who else are you expecting?"

"Calli and Tayo," Sham replied, as if Lawson should have

known.

"Why would Calli and Tayo wander your dream?" Gren's voice was filled with anxiety.

Sham shook his head. "Because they came with us. Duh!"

"Calli and Tayo are here on Abacu?" Gren's voice said, more as a statement than a question.

"Captain Fia didn't ask me anything about them," Lawson's voice commented. "So she must not know they're here."

Gren's voice grew angrier. "What were you thinking, flying halfway across the galaxy with a couple of Greens? How are they supposed to help anyone? They can't even get along for an entire unit!"

"They'd better learn to," Lawson's voice added. "They can't be caught. Not only are they our best bet to escape, but Captain Fia would just *love* to have more people who can wander."

"Neither of them can wander too far," Gren's voice said. "They tend to concentrate more on their differences than on their studies."

"Why would she want more people who can wander?" Sham asked.

"There's a war going on," Gren's voice explained. "Fia keeps asking me to wander the dreams of one of the other side's higher ups. So far, I've just wandered Lawson instead, but I think she's going to figure that out soon." She sighed. "A few dreams that come true could change the outcome of the whole conflict."

"We can't get involved," Lawson's voice said sternly. "This is *their* problem, not ours. Sham, Titus, promise us right now that you won't wander anyone's dreams but ours."

"Yeah, I guess so," Sham replied.

"Okay," Titus's voice said, "for now. But I'm not going to let them put any of us in danger."

"I wonder if Calli or Tayo is dreaming," Gren's voice said.

"Try it alone," Sham suggested, glancing around again. "Having three voices in your dream is really annoying."

Chapter Twenty-Eight

Calli stretched and yawned, then slowly opened her eyes. It took her several micros to realize where she was. She had slept better than she'd expected; all the walking must have tired her out. Her clothes were still damp, but the air was warmer than it had been. The rain had all but stopped for the time being. She stretched one more time, then lightly shook her partner's shoulder.

"Tayo, wake up."

Tayo stretched and yawned, herself. "Wow, I never thought I'd sleep like that. Where's Roy?"

"I don't think he's come back yet," Calli replied, looking around.

"I'm sure he'll be back soon," Tayo said. "He probably stopped to get some sleep. If we were that tired from walking, imagine how someone *his* age would..."

"He's not that old," Calli interrupted. "He's probably younger than my parents."

Tayo laughed. "I can't imagine your parents keeping a spaceship in their back yard."

"Well, they..." Calli stopped. She realized she was about to argue for the sake of arguing. "So you slept okay?"

"Yeah," Tayo answered. "It was weird. I kept having this dream about Gren. I could hear her, but I couldn't . . ." Tayo shook her head. "No."

Calli nodded. "I think she was trying to wander my dreams, as well. We're used to the Learning Center and a controlled environment. It never dawned on me that it might be real."

"Did you try to wander at all?" Tayo asked.

Calli put her head down, defeated. "I tried, but I couldn't find a thing. I'm not used to distances. They haven't taught us that yet. That's advanced training, even past Blue orbit. I don't know how Gren did it."

"I didn't have much luck, either. I think I entered the dream of some small animal for a micro, but since we're not supposed to wander without permission, I figure that applies even to rodents."

Calli half smiled. "Ladinda would be proud of you for that realization."

"Yeah, a lot of good that'll do us now. Are you hungry?"

"Starving," Calli replied.

Tayo opened the pack and pulled out some food. "I wonder when Roy is coming back," she said, her mouth full.

"I hope soon."

"Me, too," Tayo agreed.

Calli looked surprised. "I thought you didn't like Roy."

Tayo shook her head. "I didn't say I like him. We just don't have any more food." The slight grin on her face told Calli that Tayo was changing her mind about Roy.

"So do you remember anything about the dream?" Calli asked. "Maybe if we piece our dreams together, we can figure out what Gren was trying to tell us."

Tayo swallowed hard. "She mentioned Sham and Titus, so I guess they're with her."

"On the top floor," Calli added, looking absentmindedly into the distance. "I think she said something about being on the top floor of the army's headquarters."

"She said that to me, too," Tayo replied, her excitement growing. "She also mentioned a couple of names . . . um . . ."

"I think she said Captain Fia and Handy to me," Calli said. "They're the two people Roy mentioned."

"Yeah, but there was one other name, as well." Tayo put her head down and closed her eyes, trying to remember the dream. "Captain Fia and that Handy guy wanted her to wander someone's dream. Something about a war. The name is . . . Vo . . . Vo . . . Voder? Vomar? Something like that."

"I know what you mean, but I can't think of it, either," Calli said, feeling slightly defeated. "Maybe Roy will know. I wish he'd come back."

After two painfully slow units, it became obvious that Roy wasn't returning. Calli and Tayo were already sure that Sham and Titus had been captured...what if the same thing had happened to Roy? How long did he expect them to wait? They decided that it had been long enough.

"Which way do you think we should go?" Calli asked.

"Toward the headquarters, near where we were last night," Tayo replied. "Roy knows we've been there before, and he knows that we know Gren is there. It's the logical place to start."

"But what about the camp?" Calli asked. "That's where he was headed last night. What if he's lying on the ground, injured, waiting for us to come and help him?"

"The camp is also where Sham and Titus disappeared," Tayo reminded her. "Roy thought someone might be back. Chances are he's been caught, as well."

"Then he probably left some sort of sign for us," Calli argued. "We need to go back and look."

Tayo stared at her partner. "Do you want to break up? I'll check the headquarters, you check the camp?"

Calli shook her head. "No. Every time our group splits up,

someone disappears. But I still think..."

"Tell you what," Tayo interrupted. "Since it's closer, we'll take a good look at the headquarters first. Then, if we don't have any ideas on what to do next, we'll head back to the camp. Agreed?"

"Agreed."

Tayo grinned. "This compromise thing is easier than I thought it would be."

The trek through the woods was somewhat easier than it had been in the dark, although there were periods of rain and a couple of heavy downpours that slowed them down. By the time the army's headquarters building was in sight, both girls were drenched and hungry. "Are you sure there's no food left?" Calli asked for the fifth time.

"Roy thought he'd be back," Tayo repeated. She was just as hungry as her partner was. "I'm sure he was planning to bring something with him. But at least we can finally sit down. Now please tell me Roy didn't take the magnifiers."

"No, I have them," Calli said. She pulled them out of her pack and held them up to her eyes. "It seems pretty quiet." Without having to be asked, she handed them to Tayo.

"Yeah, you're right," Tayo agreed, looking around. "Do you think maybe we need to take a closer look?"

"Maybe," Calli said. "From this vantage point, we can only see up. There's got to be some activity on the ground. But we'll need to be careful."

"I agree." Tayo stood up and glanced around. "Hey, Calli, look! It's a jurgleberry bush! They're in season!"

"Tayo, don't!" Calli cried louder than she had planned. "They may *look* like jurgleberries, but who knows what they really are? They could be poisonous."

"Yeah, you're right," Tayo said sadly. "What would a jurgleberry bush be doing on Abacu?"

"I'm hungry, too."

"Yeah, I've noticed," Tayo teased. "You keep asking if there's any more food."

"Come on, let's try to get a closer look," Calli suggested.

They took a couple of steps forward...but something grabbed them from behind.

Chapter Twenty-Nine

"Shhh. Do not worry. We are here to be of assistance," a voice said in Calli's ear.

"We will remove ours hands if you promise not to scream," the person behind Tayo added, loud enough so that both Greens could hear.

Calli and Tayo both nodded. When the hands were removed from their mouths, they turned to face their attackers. "What is it you want from us?" Calli asked, trying to hide the fear in her voice.

"Want?" the first man repeated. He was young, although several orbits older than the two Greens, with blond hair and sparkling blue eyes. He was dressed in baggy clothes that blended in with the surroundings. "As I said, we are here to be of assistance. You looked as if you were about to head directly to the Abacuan Army Headquarters' building, and *that* is a place you do not want to go."

"We heard you mention 'jurgleberries'," the second added. He had dark skin, dark hair, and dark eyes, and appeared to be even younger than the first. His clothing was similar. "I hope you do not mean these." He pointed at the bush. "Because they are indeed poisonous."

"That was when we realized we might be able to help," the first man continued. "Our camp is not far, and we have food and dry clothing we could offer you."

Calli's stomach growled is if in answer. "Thanks," she said. She and Tayo exchanged looks. They would go, but they would be extra cautious. Calli glanced at the men's sleeves and Tayo slightly nodded. Neither man wore the Abacuan army symbol.

"Please, come this way," the first man said. He started to walk, the other three close behind him. "I am Austin," he said. "My friend is Closs."

Calli couldn't help but notice the way that both men spoke precisely, enunciating every syllable. "I'm Calli."

"And I'm Tayo."

"It is nice to meet both of you," Closs said at the rear of the group. "We are almost there. I am glad we saw you. If you had gone much closer you would have been captured."

"You do not want to be captured by the Abacuan Army," Austin chimed in.

"Why?" Calli asked. "I mean, I know it's an obvious question, but . . ."

Austin stopped. "I have heard terrible things about what happens in that building. Kidnappings. Torture. All to force someone to do what is required of them. And then . . ." He shuddered. "It is not too much farther. We have a small camp set up, away from the main one. That is where we are taking you."

"And then what happens with the army?" Tayo couldn't help but ask. "After the kidnappings and torture..."

"I have heard of many people being taken into that building who have never come out," Closs said solemnly. "It is not like that with us. Our ultimate goal is peace."

"So we're free to go?" Calli asked tentatively.

"Of course," Austin told her. "Although I thought you were hungry. There it is, up ahead."

The shapes of small tents, the same color as the men's clothes, appeared in the distance. As they grew closer, a larger tent could be seen behind the others. Austin continued to the large tent and led them inside. He grabbed some camouflaged clothes from a rack in the corner and handed them to the partners. "There are enclosures over there where you may change," he said, pointing. "Then wait here. I will bring food in a few hundreds." He and Closs left.

· ○ ◉ ● ◓ ○ ·

Neither Calli nor Tayo said anything until they'd both changed. "What do you think?" Tayo asked at last. She sat down at a table.

"Well," Calli started, "it's not quite as comfortable as our uniforms, but at least we're dry."

Tayo sighed. "I'm not talking about the clothes. If what they said is true..."

"...then Gren and Lawson are in big trouble."

"Sham and Titus, too," Tayo added. "I don't know. There's something about these people, something I think we can trust."

Calli grabbed Tayo's arm. "We can't trust *anyone* but each other right now. How do we know this isn't a trap? Maybe they're planning to use us the same way Gren and Lawson are being used."

"They don't know we're Wanderers," Tayo reminded her partner. "They don't know anything about Gren and Lawson, either. All they know is that we were close to the headquarters. That's it. And it's not like we'd be able to wander, anyway. We're only Greens, and neither of us has anything close to Gren's ability."

"Shhh," Calli warned, for Austin and Closs had returned. Both men carried plates filled with food. Another man was with them. He looked to be about the same age as Roy. He had dark hair and sad, blue eyes.

"As promised," Closs said, setting the plate in front of Calli.

He then poured her a cup of liquid.

"There is someone we would like you to meet," Austin said, after delivering Tayo's food. "Commander, these are the two campers we told you about. Their names are Calli and Tayo. Is there anything else, sir?"

"No, Austin, that will be all," the Commander replied. He sat down after the two men had left. "I hope you do not mind if I join you. It is so rare that we see new faces around here. Austin tells me you were lost in the woods."

"Yes," Calli replied, swallowing. She was even hungrier than she had thought. "We were . . .uh . . . camping. Thanks for the hospitality."

"You are not local," the Commander observed.

"No," Tayo said. She, too, was eating faster than normal. "How did you know?"

"Your accents," the Commander informed her. "You do not speak the same way the local residents do. They also do not often venture out into the woods. Forgive me for saying so, but two girls camping in unfamiliar surroundings does not seem very wise, especially since you did not bring adequate supplies with you. Is there anything I can help you with?"

"No, thank you," Calli responded. "The food and the dry clothes are more than enough, Commander."

The Commander smiled. "You do not need to call me that; you are not under my command. Please, my name is Vomat."

Calli and Tayo exchanged glances, both realizing *Vomat* was the name Gren had tried to tell them in their sleep.

"I think you will like the clothing," Vomat continued. "It is water repellant, which would be better for camping. Although I cannot see why anyone would choose to spend one micro more than they had to in this miserable area."

"You're not from around here?" Tayo asked tentatively.

Vomat shook his head. "Oh, no. We arrived here over two orbits ago. We were sent from Eden as a peace envoy. Unfortunately, we were shot down and our ship was destroyed. The General is not interested in peace."

"The General?" Calli repeated.

"If you did not already know, you would have found out about him had Austin and Closs not stopped you," Vomat informed them. "As I said, he is not interested in peace. He wants the war to continue for his own personal gain." Vomat yawned. "Please forgive me. My sleep has not been normal lately. I do not understand why."

"Tell me about it," Tayo suggested curiously. "Calli and I know a little bit about sleep disorders. Maybe we can offer some suggestions."

Vomat seemed embarrassed. "I have fallen asleep at some very unusual times. In the evening, after the meal, I have become extremely tired, unable to stay awake. Immediately I have been plagued by terrible dreams. It does not last long, but it makes it difficult to sleep at the correct time. But I do not understand how two young girls could expect to help..."

"Sleep tonic," Tayo muttered, cutting him off.

"Tayo, don't," Calli warned.

"Calli, you trusted Roy based on your instincts. I feel the same way now," Tayo stated. "We're going to need help; we can't pull this off on our own."

Calli nodded slowly.

Tayo continued: "Vomat, has there been anything else unusual? Who has prepared your meal or, more importantly, what you drink with it? And besides us, has there been anyone new around here lately?"

"There is a young girl," Vomat replied. "A runaway slave child. I cannot stand to see the way they treat those children. Forced into labor for the smallest of offenses. She has been helping out, trying to feel needed."

"During these dreams, has anyone tried to talk to you?" Tayo asked. "Talk you through the bad parts?"

"I do not understand," Vomat answered.

"Gren said she was *supposed* to deliver a message," Calli reminded Tayo. "I doubt she actually did. Wandering without permission is illegal *and* immoral. Gren wouldn't break the law unless it was a last resort."

"You're right," Tayo agreed.

"Austin mentioned that this isn't your main camp," Calli said. "How long have you been here? And why did you move?"

Poor Vomat looked extremely confused. "We were attacked earlier. No one was injured; we were able to escape. We do not think the army knows where this camp is located. We do not want to fight them, but they keep coming after us. Their attacks have been more frequent the past few rotations. What does this have to do with my dreams?"

Tayo looked directly at her partner, who nodded. "You're right, Vomat, we're not from around here. We live on Terra."

Vomat laughed. "Terra? It is uninhabited."

"No," Calli said, shaking her head. "We're also peaceful people, and until a few rotations ago neither of us realized there was life elsewhere in the galaxy."

"Have they attacked your planet too?" Vomat asked, worried. "The Abacuan Army?"

"They didn't attack the planet," Tayo explained. "But they did kidnap a couple of our friends. And you were given sleep tonic. That's why you're having the bad dreams."

"I do not understand," Vomat said. "What would the army want with your friends? And what is this 'sleep tonic' you keep mentioning?"

Tayo thought for several micros, realizing how crazy it must all sound. "We're Dream Wandering students. We're learning to enter people's dreams, especially their nightmares."

"It's a form of therapy," Calli interjected. "We talk someone through a dream and calm their fears, or we help them break bad habits."

"It's surprisingly effective," Tayo added.

"We're just students," Calli threw in. "Tayo and I have a long way to go before we earn our licenses."

"But our friend Gren," Tayo continued, "who's older than we are, has remarkable abilities. She and Lawson..."

"Her partner..."

"Gren and Lawson, her partner, disappeared from the Learning Center a few rotations ago. Some sleep tonic was stolen, as well."

"One type of sleep tonic makes the drinker fall asleep and have terrible dreams," Calli explained. "The Wanderer then talks the sleeper through their fears. The system workers thought Lawson stole the tonic, but we knew he hadn't."

"The whole thing is a long story," Tayo continued, "but we found out Gren and Lawson were here. We came with two other students..."

"Sham and Titus..."

"Sham and Titus, but they've disappeared, as well, and we're pretty sure that they've also been captured. And who knows what's happened to Roy?"

"What does this have to do with my dreams?" Vomat was having an extremely hard time keeping up with the conversation. "And who is Roy?"

"Roy is a friend of Sham's," Tayo said. "He flew us here."

"And it looks like someone has been slipping you sleep tonic," Calli explained. "Gren is supposed to give you messages in your dreams...that's what the army has been asking her to do...but I don't think she's been doing it. There's a strict legal and moral code when it comes to wandering. I don't know what the messages are, but it looks like someone is trying to manipulate you."

"And you are sure your friends were kidnapped by the army?"

Tayo nodded. "We saw Gren on the roof of the headquarters' building last night. She was with a woman that Roy claimed was in the army. We think her name is Fia."

"Captain Fia." Vomat nodded. "There is then one thing I must do."

"What?" Calli and Tayo asked in unison.

"Help you to rescue your friends."

Chapter Thirty

Gren wasn't surprised when Captain Fia took her to the roof for a third time. She was tired; she had spent so much time trying to find her friends and their dreams that she had slept little herself. She couldn't wait for it to be all over. She wanted to be back at the Learning Center, talking with her roommates or sitting by the tree near the lake with Lawson. Part of her doubted those things would ever happen again. If they survived and actually returned home, there would be so much to explain. Sham and Titus would help. She thought Roy probably would, as well, even though she hadn't met him. She just hoped he would be believable, not come off as crazy.

Fia led Gren to the same spot. "I wish the rain would stop," Fia said. "That's one of the things I miss about Terra, the weather. Once the war is over, maybe I'll be able to return. Maybe I'll . . . I'm getting ahead of myself here."

"What's the message this time?" Gren asked. She hadn't really been paying attention to what Fia said.

"You're certainly getting used to this!" Fia replied with a grin.

"Will I be able to see Lawson again?" Gren asked. She had almost mentioned Titus and Sham, but then she remembered she wasn't supposed to know they were there.

Fia was noncommittal. "We'll see. Maybe. Or maybe I'll have a different surprise for you. Now, we need a message that will really grab Vomat's attention. Something that will cause him to take us more seriously." She paused for several micros. A smile spread across her face. "I know. How about, 'Tomorrow will be a rotation of peace'? That's one message that will make him happy when it comes true. And then . . ." She stopped.

"What?" Gren asked nervously. She was starting to understand. If Vomat believed what she said, eventually she would be forced to deceive him by delivering wrong information. She was pretty sure they weren't at that point yet. A rotation of peace was probably what the commander could expect.

"Don't your worry your pretty little head about it," Fia responded. "Hold on." She fiddled with the communicator. "Okay, all set. Wander Vomat's dream and deliver the message."

"'Tomorrow will be a rotation of peace,'" Gren repeated.

"Right."

Gren closed her eyes and concentrated. She reached out. She planned to touch Vomat's dream, as she had before, just enough so that if they were testing her she would know. Then, she would give the message to Lawson. She continued to search; the location was different from before. Finally, she found the trace of sleep tonic. She wandered to the edge of the dream and, without meaning to, sighed.

"Gren!" two female voices shouted in unison.

As a reflex Gren visibly jumped. She tried to maintain contact. The dream came into focus; they were on some sort of giant ship. Vomat was at the controls; Gren recognized him from his picture. It was obvious that the ship was about to crash. "What's going on?" Gren's voice asked.

"Gren, it's us," Calli's voice said quickly. "We're here with Vomat. He's going to help us rescue you. If you have a message for him go ahead and give it...you need to keep up appearances."

"'Tomorrow will be a rotation of peace.'"

"Listen, Gren," Tayo's voice said, "I know you don't have much time. When you get a chance, try to wander Calli or me. We're going to take turns sleeping. Neither of us is strong enough to wander distances."

"I have to go," Gren's voice said. "I'll try later, but it will probably be a couple of units." Opening her eyes, Gren broke contact.

Captain Fia was furious. "What happened?"

Gren pretended she didn't know what Fia was talking about. "What happened with what?"

Fia stared at Gren. "Something startled you. You jumped. And you took a lot longer than normal. Come on, Gren, *what happened*?"

"It took longer because I couldn't find him. They were in a different location. And I jumped because . . ." she looked down, trying to buy time.

"Because why, Gren?"

"The dream," Gren lied. "It was terrible! A giant ship had lost control, and I showed up right when it hit the ground! I'm only a student, you know. If I see something terrible like that, I can't help but react."

"Oh," Fia said, buying the story. "That must have been a terrible surprise."

"Was it true?" Gren asked. "Was Vomat really piloting a giant ship that crashed?"

"He came here to attack our headquarters," Fia explained. "We defended ourselves, and his ship was destroyed. He and his forces have set up one large and several smaller camps in the area. They attack us every chance they get."

Gren was confused. "But the two previous messages...both

times Vomat was warned of an upcoming assault. He wasn't doing the attacking."

"An offensive move, Gren," Fia told her, "which was also defensive. Sometimes we need to make our move before they can make theirs."

"May I ask you something?"

"You may ask me anything," Fia replied. "That doesn't mean I'll answer."

Gren swallowed hard. She was trusting Fia less all the time, and a lot depended on her answer. "How am I helping to end the war?"

Fia smiled as sweetly as possible. "Don't even think about the war. That's my problem. Come." She put a hand and Gren's back and nudged her gently forward. "Let me show you that surprise. And Lawson can be there, too."

As Gren walked back toward the elevator, she decided defiitively that Fia was lying to her. She was being asked to help the wrong side of the war.

As happy as she was to see Lawson, Gren wished she could just go back to her cell. There were things she wanted to discuss with Lawson, but only in his dreams. Gren pretended to be surprised to see Titus and Sham, since she wasn't supposed to know they were there. She only partially listened to their "official" story of their arrival. They were hard to understand, because of the enormous amounts of food they were consuming.

Gren continued to think about what Fia had said. The woman hadn't really told her anything. And there was something in both Calli's and Tayo's voices. They seemed to trust this Vomat person. A person who'd said he would help. She didn't know much about him but the idea that a total stranger would be willing to assist in a rescue, a rescue necessary because they had been kidnapped by Captain Fia . . .

"You look tired, Lawson," Gren said, interrupting Titus.

Lawson immediately picked up on her clue. Gren had to tell him something important, so he needed to dream again as soon as the meal was over. "You'd be tired too, listening to Sham snoring all night."

"How could I have been snoring all night?" Sham objected. "You made us sleep on the floor!"

"Believe me, Sham, you were snoring," Titus told him.

"It's not my fault," Sham said, feigning hurt. "People can't help what they do when they sleep. I don't know, it's like dreaming. You can't control what you dream."

"But we control other people's dreams, to a certain extent," Gren mumbled.

Lawson looked at her. "Another message for Vomat?" He was surprised. She had given him the previous messages, but he hadn't received the latest one.

Gren nodded. "'Tomorrow will be a rotation of peace.' That's a good message, isn't it? Maybe it means the war is almost over and we'll be able to return home soon." Gren heard the door open but pretended to ignore it. "We're really helping to bring peace to the planet. At first I was upset about the whole situation, but now I'm glad we're here. We have an opportunity to make a difference in thousands of lives. It's quite an honor, really."

"It's good to hear you speak that way, Gren," Captain Fia said at the door. Handy stood behind her. "I told you before; your name will be remembered by our people. But we're not there yet, and it's time to go back."

"Back to Terra?" Sham asked with hope.

Handy shook his head. "It took these two long enough to come around, but now I've got to put up with two more of ya? You're goin' back to the cell, which ya already knew."

"Can't blame him for wishful thinking," Lawson said.

A few hundreds later, Gren quickly wandered into Lawson's dream. He was once again in his dorm room. She was in such a hurry that she didn't even pay attention to the surroundings. "Sham, Titus, you here too?" her voice asked.

"Yeah, both of us," Titus's voice replied.

"Good. Listen, I've been in contact with Calli and Tayo. They're both fine. I was only able to talk to them for a micro, because it happened when I was wandering Vomat's dream. He's going to help rescue us. I'm going to try to contact them now."

"Gren," Sham's voice said, "did they say anything about Roy?"

"No," Gren's voice replied. "I'll make sure I ask them. Anything else?"

"I don't think so," Sham's voice said.

"Okay." Gren's voice sighed. "I'll come back here as soon as I find something out. Try to take turns sleeping."

Lawson looked around. "When are *you* going to get some sleep, Gren?"

Gren's voice sighed again. "Who knows?"

Soon Gren found herself in another dorm room, one she knew extremely well. Calli sat on her bed. No one else was visible in the room. Immediately, Gren realized something was wrong. Calli was crying.

"Calli?" Gren's voice said softly.

"I thought you weren't supposed to call people by name when wandering," Tayo's voice reminded her. "That's what

Charla always told us."

"Charla and Hutch are both wrong," Gren's voice said. "At least, that's what Lawson and I have found out. Maybe you shouldn't do it in a therapy session, but among friends it seems to help. Calli, why are you crying?"

"It's happened again," Calli mumbled. "I knew it would."

"What?" Gren's voice wanted to know, but Calli refused to answer.

"So what's going on, Gren?" Tayo's voice asked at last.

"Here's the short version," Gren's voice started. "Lawson and I were kidnapped. There are two main people we've been dealing with, Captain Fia and Handy. Fia told me that we're going to help end the war. I'm supposed to wander this Vomat person's dreams and give him messages, but I haven't been doing it. Fia said that Vomat and the people with him came to attack the army's headquarters."

Calli ignored the voices in her head and continued to mumble.

"Vomat told us he was part of a peace envoy," Tayo's voice informed her. "They were shot down."

"After seeing his dream, that's what I thought," Gren's voice agreed. She paused. "Do you trust Vomat?"

"Yeah," Tayo's voice replied without hesitation. "His friends brought us to his camp. They fed us and he offered to help without our even asking. I don't know what it is about him, but I do trust him. Gren, have you heard anything about Sham or Titus? I know you mentioned them last night, but neither Calli nor I realized that we were being wandered."

"I've seen them," Gren's voice told her. "They're here. It didn't take them long to be captured. Sham wanted me to ask about Roy. Is he with you?"

"I thought he'd be with you," Tayo's voice said. "Well, he knows the area. I'm sure he's fine."

"It's happened again," Calli said.

"So what do we do now?" Gren's voice asked.

"Vomat said to sit tight. He's working on a rescue plan. Any information you could give us would be useful."

"We're on the top floor. Lawson is staying down the hall from me. Oh, and I almost forgot!" The smile could be heard in Gren's voice. "Zero-six-one-one."

"Zero-six-one-one," Tayo's voice repeated. "What's that?"

"That," Gren's voice said with quite a bit of satisfaction, "is Captain Fia's code. I've watched her use it in a couple of different places, and it's always the same."

"Wow, good work Gren!" Tayo's voice remarked. "So, how do we get in touch with you?"

"Since you two can't wander distances," Gren's voice started, "and apparently neither can any of the boys, I'll just keep reaching out from time to time. But try, anyway; with a little bit of practice, it's not really all that hard. And once you get closer, Lawson has perfected the art of letting his mind wander, so you can always contact him, although you have to promise not to use anything he's dreaming against us."

"It's not too hard to figure out who *his* dreams are about," Tayo's voice teased. She then grew more serious. "Don't worry, Gren, we'll be back at the Learning Center soon."

"Thanks." Gren sounded grateful for the encouragement.

"I knew it would happen again, but I can't believe it has," Calli mumbled.

In the dream, the door opened and Gren walked in. She sat on the bed next to her. "Calli, you're crying!" the dream-Gren noticed. "What's wrong?"

"I don't know how I'm going to tell my parents," Calli said. "It's happened again."

"What?" the dream-Gren asked.

"Tayo and I are no longer partners," Calli said sadly. "Ladinda didn't think it was working. Tayo's already been reassigned, but if they can't find a new Green for me, I'm out of the program."

The dream-Gren put an arm around Calli. "They'll find someone. Don't worry."

Calli sighed. "The worst part is that I really like Tayo. I know we fight a lot, but I think that's just because we both put up all these stupid defenses. Losing a partner is really hard, and I think I've been trying to hurt her before she could hurt me. Only it backfired."

"Did you try telling this to Ladinda?" the dream-Gren asked.

"No," Calli replied. She wiped her eyes. "What really stinks is that Tayo is the best friend I've ever had. I can't tell her that now... she obviously hates me. I guess she'll never know."

"I don't hate you," Tayo's voice said in the dream. "You're my best friend, too."

Chapter Thirty-One

After a good night's sleep, Tayo and Calli washed up for the morning meal. Tayo was having a hard time looking Calli in the eye. "Listen, Calli, about last night..."

"Look, it's no one's fault if we both fell asleep," Calli reassured her. "I know it would have been better if one of us had stayed awake so we could try to wander with Gren, but sometimes your body just shuts itself down. I wonder if Gren tried. She sounded kind of tired."

Tayo looked puzzled. "You don't remember?"

"Remember what?"

"Gren and I *did* wander your dream," Tayo explained.

Calli shook her head. "I don't remember a thing. I didn't do anything embarrassing, did I?" "No," said Tayo, a little too quickly. "In fact, Gren and I pretty much ignored you. We just talked."

"Did you find out anything definite about Sham and Titus?"

"They're there." Tayo sighed. "Gren has seen both of them. But she doesn't know anything about Roy."

"I hope he's okay," Calli said.

Austin appeared at the entrance to the tent. "Ladies, if you will come with me, your meal has been prepared for you. Commander Vomat will join you when you are done."

The meal was served in the large tent. For most of it, Calli and Tayo were alone. Tayo told her partner everything Gren had said. She didn't mention what happened in the dream, although she couldn't help but think about it. They also discussed their situation. They knew their only chance of rescuing their friends was to trust Vomat and his people. They hoped they weren't making a mistake.

Not too long after they had finished eating and the dishes had been cleared away, they were joined by Vomat, Austin, and Closs. "I trust that our accommodations were suitable," Vomat said at once. "We may not have much to offer, but what we do have we are willing to share."

"Everything was fine," Tayo replied.

"Thank you," Calli added.

"Did you have any luck contacting your friend?" Vomat asked. "I still do not understand the concept of dream wandering. We do not have anything like it at home."

"I talked to Gren," Tayo said. "Calli was asleep and doesn't remember. Dreams are easier to remember if you wake up right away. Gren told me that she and Lawson were brought here to wander your dreams, Vomat. Until last night, she hadn't been doing it. They've been giving her messages to pass on to you."

"For example, the message about a rotation of peace," Vomat said.

"Yes," Tayo continued. "I guess they think that if you have enough dreams come true, you'll start to believe them. Then they'd give you something that's the opposite of their real plans..."

"And wipe us out," Austin mumbled.

"Does it work both ways?" Closs asked. "Could you give messages to Captain Fia?"

"Not without her permission," Calli said quickly. "There are all kinds of legal and moral rules that we can't break."

"We would never ask you to do something that you feel is morally wrong," Vomat assured her. "It would not be a good idea, anyway. Fia is not stupid. She would know that you are here. I do not wish to put you in any further danger."

"Any further . . ." Tayo repeated, her nervousness showing.

Vomat didn't elaborate. "Did you learn anything that might be useful to us?"

"Oh," Tayo replied, slightly embarrassed. "I almost forgot. Gren gave me Captain Fia's personal code."

"And it is?"

Tayo paused. If she gave Vomat the information, it meant that they trusted him completely. Something about him told her it was the right thing to do. She took a deep breath and glanced at Calli, who nodded. "Zero-six-one-one."

"Zero-six-one-one," Vomat repeated. "That will help a great deal. Austin, Closs, gather some supplies. The three of us shall leave for the headquarters right away."

"The *three* of you?" The surprise was obvious in Calli's voice. "We're going with you!"

"No," Vomat said. "It is too dangerous. You will be safer here, especially since we know that this is a rotation of peace."

"What if *that* was the wrong message?" Tayo argued. "We just agreed that sometime it's going to be a lie. Claiming there will be peace would cause you to let down your guard, wouldn't it? We'll be no safer here than with you."

"Plus you don't know anything about wandering," Calli added. "Once we get closer, Tayo and I might be able to find out more information from our friends. We could be really helpful to you." She knew that neither she nor Tayo was yet capable of doing what she'd implied, but she didn't care. She wasn't going to let them go without her.

"If we don't go with you, we'll go on our own," Tayo promised. "You can't keep us here."

"We could . . ." Austin started.

"But we will not," Vomat added right away. "All right, you may accompany us, but I will expect you to do as you are told. Do not second-guess us. The Royal Abacuan Army is filled with ruthless individuals; they will think nothing of harming or even killing you. Do you understand?"

"Yes . . . sir," Calli and Tayo quietly replied in unison.

"Good. We will leave in ten hundreds. Austin, Closs, the supplies. Just the basics. This should not take long."

Less than a unit later, they were again walking through the woods. Tayo was thankful for their new, water-repellent clothes; the constant rain didn't bother her quite as much as before. She talked a bit with Closs as they walked.

"Not long after we crashed here, we discovered a plant," he explained. "We had never seen anything like it before. It grows deep within the woods. It is similar to a bush, I suppose, although it has only one large leaf, covering the entire plant. The leaf is shed several times an orbit. We harvest the leaves and, since they are large, they are suitable for making clothing."

"What do you do for food?" Tayo asked. "Where do you find it?"

"We grow it," Closs answered. "At the main camp. We were lucky enough to have had seeds within our supplies when we arrived, and the plants seem to like the soil. They grow better here than they ever did at home."

"What's it like?" Tayo wanted to know. "Eden, I mean."

Closs sighed. "It is the most beautiful place you can imagine. The air is clean and crisp. The sky is the most incredible shade of light purple. Water flows freely; there are streams with waterfalls covering the planet. Trees, flowers, birds . . ."

"It is a very peaceful place," Austin added. He was walking

nearby. "There is one city with a manufacturing center, but the rest is rural."

"Our people were very happy," Closs continued, "until..."

"There is no need to burden Tayo with our problems," Vomat interrupted from the head of the group. "We need not bring them into our war. It is not their fight."

"But Commander," Closs pleaded, "if they have a..."

Vomat stopped, turned around, and stared at Closs, who didn't say another word. After several micros, the group started hiking again.

Calli moved forward, walking closer to Vomat. She thought to a hundred than asked, "What do we have that you want?"

"Nothing," Vomat replied, picking up the pace slightly. "I think Closs was referring to your ship, that perhaps a message could be sent from it back to our home. But I do not want to put more of my people in danger. We will find another way."

"But you're helping us," Calli said. "If there's anything we can do to return the favor . . ."

"Before we talk of returning favors, we need to rescue your friends," Vomat reminded her. He stopped walking again. "We are there."

Calli glanced around, seeing nothing but trees and bushes. "Where?" She pointed. "I thought the headquarters was over in that direction."

Vomat, Austin and Closs all ignored her. Instead they started to dig. Before long, something metal appeared, set in the ground. Calli and Tayo watched in amazement as a hatch came into view. Closs turned on a small light and entered first. He reappeared within micros. "It is all clear, Commander."

Austin turned on his light, then lowered himself in, followed by the two Greens. Vomat was the last inside. He shut the hatch behind him. He pulled out three more small lights, handed one to each girl, and kept the last for himself. "This is also an entrance. The army does not seem to use it. Follow Austin and Closs, and stay close."

Guided by the small lights, the group of five headed down the dark, damp corridor.

Chapter Thirty-Two

The long, winding corridor seemed like it would never end. The air was heavy, hot, and musty. The floor was covered by a thick layer of dust, making their tracks obvious even in the dark. There were other footprints, as well.

"We have been down here several times since discovering the entrance," Vomat explained, his voice just above a whisper. "It seems to be a forgotten path, or maybe they just do not think they need it any more."

"Ewww," Calli said with a shiver. "Tayo, in your hair..."

"What?" Tayo asked nervously.

"Hold still," Calli instructed. She removed a large black insect and part of a web from the back of Tayo's head.

Tayo stared at the creature. "I think I'm going to be sick . . ."

"Do not worry," Closs informed her. "It is only a jick. It will not hurt you; they are not poisonous."

"But it's ugly . . ."

"With all those eyes, just imagine how you must look to it!" Calli teased.

"Come, we must continue," Vomat said. "I would think that finding your friends is more important than the study of insects."

"It is," Calli said, slightly ashamed. "I'm sorry." She wasn't really sure what she had done wrong, but she was embarrassed.

"There is still a long way," Vomat said. "We must keep up our pace."

· ○ ○ ● ◐ ○ ○ ·

A dirty half-unit later, they stopped and sat down on the

dusty floor. Without being told, Austin opened a bag and passed out some food. As they ate, they discussed plans.

"You are sure they are on the top floor?" Vomat asked the two girls.

"Gren said that to both of us," Calli replied.

"She repeated it when we were wandering Calli's dream," Tayo added.

"That is where we have come to believe the holding cells are," Austin said.

"It has just been confirmed." Vomat looked directly at the two men with him. "We will not use the lift. It is too public and therefore too dangerous." He drew a rough sketch of the building in the dust on the ground. "Our intelligence has shown there are two stairwells. Neither runs the entire height of the building. We are here . . ." He made a mark in the dust. "The lower stairwell is here." He made another mark on the other side of the dust-building. "That leads to the fifth floor, when once again we will need to cross the length of the building to reach the stairwell that is here." The mark showed they would have to crisscross the building again. "That should lead to the top floor. The cells are to the left of the door through which we will exit, although according to our intelligence there are some cells at the opposite end of the hall."

"Sir, what if our intelligence is wrong?" Austin asked slowly.

"Then we will make up a new plan as we go along," Vomat replied, a hint of a smile on his face. He opened a bag and pulled out three dark green bags. He handed one to each of his men and held onto the third one himself. "Just in case," he said.

Calli stared for several micros, realizing what was happening. "Wait a hundred, what about Tayo and me?"

"You are to stay here," Vomat told her. "You will be much safer."

"But we didn't . . ." Tayo paused. She didn't want to sound whiny. "You don't know who we're looking for. You have no idea what Gren looks like."

"And as we said before," Calli added, "you might need us to wander. We can at least try to find out if anything's going on."

"Show me again," Vomat instructed.

"Excuse me?" Calli replied.

"Try to wander," Vomat explained. "You keep telling me that it could be useful. Try to wander right now, see if you can find out any information from your friends. Otherwise, you will wait here."

Calli and Tayo exchanged glances. Neither of them had ever wandered the dream of someone who wasn't right in front of them. It seemed impossible. Then again, Gren could do it, and she was only an orbit older than they were.

Calli sighed, stood up, and wiped off some of the dirt. "Okay," she said. Tayo followed. They faced each other, joined hands, and closed their eyes.

"This is crazy," Austin said. Neither Calli nor Tayo reacted. He looked at Vomat. "They do not seem to be doing anything."

"They also do not seem to hear you," Closs pointed out.

"Quiet," Vomat ordered. "Although I do not understand what they are attempting, we have to allow them to try."

The three men sat there, staring at the two girls. Occasionally one of the Greens would move her mouth as if to talk, but no words were formed. At the same time, they both opened their eyes. "Sham and Titus are in the same room as Lawson," Calli said excitedly.

"Gren is by herself," Tayo added. "She's way down the hall,

in the other direction."

"They still haven't seen Roy," Calli said sadly.

"Most importantly," Tayo continued, "we also now have Handy's code. It's seven-one-nine-zero."

"Handy has spent more time with the guys than Fia has," Calli said, although that bit of information didn't seem to be necessary.

Vomat looked impressed. "So you wandered and were able to communicate with Gren."

"No," Tayo replied. "Gren was asleep, but Lawson was dreaming. We actually spoke with Sham and Titus through Lawson's dream."

"So you see, we *can* be useful," Calli said.

"You may come," Vomat said. "But you will do exactly as I say, and you will stay with me unless otherwise ordered."

"Okay," Calli promised.

"I do not understand," Austin said. "If Gren was asleep, why did you not wander her?"

"There are different levels of sleep," Calli explained. "You don't dream in all of them. Gren is exhausted from always trying to contact everyone. She's sleeping way too deeply to dream."

Vomat opened the pack and pulled out two more bags. He handed one to each girl. "These are for you. You are to keep them sealed until I tell you otherwise." He opened his own green bag and took out what looked like a white rag. Austin and Closs followed suit.

"What are these for?" Tayo asked.

"Subduing the enemy," Closs replied.

Vomat stared hard at him for several hundreds. He then turned his attention back toward the girls. "We will not hurt anyone," he said at last. "It is called a sleeper. It is to be placed over someone's nose and mouth, to knock them out temporarily. Make sure you do not breathe it in yourself...it is very powerful."

Calli and Tayo nodded nervously.

"Do you have any questions?" Vomat asked.

"No, sir."

"Then we will begin." Vomat shone his light toward a well-hidden door. "Austin, you are to go first, followed by Closs. After you give the signal, I will enter with the two girls." He shone the light on the door's small panel. "Zero-six-one-one," he said out loud. With a loud creak, the door slowly opened.

Chapter Thirty-Three

It took several micros for their eyes to adjust to the light. Everyone unconsciously held their breath and listened for footsteps or any sign that others were around. Austin looked at Vomat, who nodded. Positioning the rag in the center of his hand, Austin went through the door and to the left. Closs immediately followed but went right. Less than a hundred later, Closs reemerged. "There is no one in the immediate vicinity," he informed his commander.

Calli and Tayo went through the door, Vomat behind them. He closed the door. They were in a stark, barren corridor. It was the opposite of where they had just been. The floor, ceiling, and walls were all dazzling white, and there wasn't a speck of dirt to be found. A continuous bright light shone overhead; it stretched over the entire ceiling. The girls looked around; they had never seen anything quite like it before. "It looks like something you might see in somebody's dream," Calli said, with awe in her voice.

"This way," Austin said. He took off at a run, reminding them of their task. The rest of the group followed him. They past several doors along the way; most were marked as supply rooms. Finally, they stopped. "Is this it, sir?"

"It should be," Vomat replied, "if our intelligence is correct. The stairwell should be the next door we come to. We will follow the same procedure as before."

Closs glanced at the keypad. "Which code should we use?"

"Since we have two codes, we should probably use them both," Vomat answered. "Let us see if Handy's works, as well.

As a precaution: if we are separated, you and Austin are to use Handy's code; the girls and I will use the other one."

"Yes, sir," Closs replied. Making sure everyone was in position, Closs pressed the numbers. The door opened, and Austin ran through.

"Hey!" A surprised guard turned around and pointed a stick at Austin. Closs had already snuck around behind the man and put the rag over his mouth. The guard's body immediately went limp. Closs carefully pulled the man into the corridor and gently laid him on the floor. Austin picked up the stick, broke it in two over his knee, and placed it near the sleeping guard.

"He is fine," Vomat informed the partners. "He will sleep for several units, but he will suffer no ill effects."

For a second time, Austin went through the open door, Closs right behind. They declared all clear, and the rest followed. As the door to the corridor hummed closed, the guard could be heard mumbling in his sleep.

"There," Vomat said. He pointed at another door. "That should be the stairwell."

No code was required for the stairs. They continued with the same course of action: Austin first, followed by Closs, Calli and Tayo together, and Vomat as rear guard. As quietly as possible, they started up the stairs. The white metal carried noise, so they walked on the tips of their toes. Five stories took their toll on the girls, whose legs grew exhausted, but neither one complained.

When they reached the fifth floor, Vomat huddled them into a group. "This will be tricky," he whispered. "We need to cross the length of the building. This floor will not be like the other; it could be busy. Try not to be seen...but if you are, do your best to look as though you belong here." He paused, knowing that suggestion was next to impossible.

"There should be plenty of places to hide. If you give anyone the sleeper, make sure you place that person somewhere that they will not be quickly found. And this goes without saying, but if you are caught, do not tell them what our objective is. Tell them that you were looking for their communications center so you could try to send a message home. Remember, we are here to rescue the kidnapped students. If anything does go wrong, we will rectify it later, but now we must complete our mission."

"Why are you talking like something might go wrong?" Tayo asked.

"Because, my friend, there is a very good chance that something will."

Taking it quite a bit slower than they had before, Austin opened the stairwell door and slipped out. A micro later there was a soft, high-pitched whistle. Closs barely opened the door and snuck out. Another whistle, and Vomat followed. The partners were close behind. They had entered another corridor, this one less stark white than before.

Austin took a few steps forward, then ducked into a doorway. The others followed. Slowly, quietly, they made their way along.

Suddenly, Austin held up a hand. Everyone stopped. He put a finger to his lips; some people could be heard talking. Austin motioned to show that they were close by. He went down on his hands and knees and crawled across the floor. He stopped and then motioned for the others to join him. One by one, they crawled along.

Calli's hands were shaking, and her heart was pounding so loudly she was sure it could be heard.

"Aw come on," a man's voice said. "I'm not askin' ya to be joined or nothin'. Just one meal! Does the idea of one meal with me really bother ya that much?"

A woman giggled. "No, not *that* much." She giggled again. "But, ya know, people talk. I don't wanna become the new topic of gossip around this place."

"Who cares what anyone else thinks?" the man asked. "If ya like me, we should . . ."

Calli had made it past; she didn't care that she would never hear the end of the exchange. The group continued, ducking into doorways, crawling past desks, hearing parts of conversations. It seemed to take an eternity to make it to the other side of the building. Finally, Austin pointed to a door.

Calli's heart leapt for joy; it must be the other stairwell. It wouldn't be long until they were on the top floor, rescuing Gren, Lawson, and the others.

Vomat ducked into a doorway and signaled for the two girls to join him. "That is it," he whispered. He nodded at Austin, who nodded back, glanced around, and started toward the door.

"Stop!" a man ordered. "Hands up!" He pointed a stick at Austin.

Austin raised his hands. Closs moved into position, sneaking around the man as he had before. As he reached to put his hand over the man's nose and mouth, a second man appeared. "I wouldn't if I were ya," the second man said calmly, placing something in the center of Closs's back. "I need ya to raise your hands, as well."

Prepared for the possibility of being caught, both men subtly allowed their white rags to slip into their sleeves unnoticed.

"What are ya doin' here?" the first man asked.

"I will not tell *you*," Austin answered. "I will speak only with your superiors."

"*I will speak only with your superiors,*" the second mocked. He turned to Closs. "What were ya doin' there before? What were ya gonna do to Scratch?"

"Scratch?" Austin repeated, letting out a small laugh. "What kind of name is Scratch? Did your parents think you were a feline of some type? Or were you born with an itch?" His laugh grew louder.

"Don't ya make fun of my name *or* my parents!" Scratch yelled. "Why I should just..."

Without wasting any time, Austin took a swing at Scratch, while Closs took on the other man. Soon, an all-out, hand-to-hand battle raged.

"Now is our chance, go!" Vomat whispered.

Surprised, Calli and Tayo darted toward the door and the second stairwell. Vomat followed. "They have bought us some time."

"Shouldn't we wait for them?" Calli asked.

Vomat shook his head. "They are acting as a decoy. They will fight for several hundreds, and then lose the battle. While the base deals with them, we should be able to make it to your friends with a lot less hassle."

"But..." Tayo objected, not able to put her feelings into words.

"If they are not able to escape on their own, I will come back for them. I promise. And I will return with some of my best people, not two young girls. Hurry, we are wasting valuable time. Do not let their sacrifice be in vain."

"Sacrifice," Tayo repeated quietly to herself, not liking the sound of the word one bit.

The door from the stairwell to the top floor was coded. "This is a restricted area," Vomat explained. "Even their own people are not allowed here without clearance. It is a good thing we have Captain Fia's code." He placed his finger near the keypad. "When the door opens, you will wait. I will make sure that all is clear."

Vomat pressed the numbers. The lock unlatched, and the door opened slightly. He opened it a little bit more and looked through the crack. He opened it further and slipped through. "This way," he said quietly.

He eased his way along the wall, the two Greens following. They traveled a good way across the building. Finally, Vomat stopped and pointed. "Around the corner and to the left is where the cells should be. He placed the white rag in the center of his hand. "Have your sleepers ready."

The girls ripped open the bags and pulled out the rags. Vomat peered around the corner. "It looks clear, but wait for my signal."

Vomat snuck around the corner and took a couple of steps forward. Calli was preparing to follow when she heard a man's voice. "Hands up!"

"I am lost." Vomat said calmly. "I was looking for Internal Affairs. Is it on this floor?"

"I know exactly who you are," a woman's voice said. "Commander Vomat. How nice of you to join us. The General will be pleased. Very pleased indeed."

Calli and Tayo listened from around the corner, not sure what they should do. They glanced at each other and made sure their sleepers were ready.

"Captain Fia, it is nice to finally meet you in person," Vomat said. "There is no need to involve the General. If you would just show me your Communications Center, I will contact my planet, and this pesky little conflict will finally be over."

"Contact your planet *and* their armada?" Fia asked. "I don't think so."

"Captain, what do ya want me to do?" the man's voice asked.

"As I said, Handy, the General will be pleased. Take him. Now!"

Calli and Tayo listened intently. A few footsteps could be heard, followed by the beginning of a scuffle. They came out from around the corner in time to see a blast aimed at Vomat. Calli ran behind Handy, Tayo behind Captain Fia, and both placed the rags over their mouths. Handy and Fia collapsed, unconscious, almost taking the partners down with them.

"Make sure they are out of sight," Vomat said. His voice was strained. The two Greens dragged their sleeping captives to a closet and put them inside.

"Wow," said Tayo, letting out a deep breath. "I hope we don't have to do anything like that again."

"I agree." Calli was shaking, obviously filled with adrenaline. "Commander Vomat, what do we do now?"

There was no answer. Calli and Tayo glanced at each other, then rushed to Vomat's side. He lay on the floor under a desk. He held his hands over his stomach, his shirt was red. He was fighting for each breath. "The two of you . . . are strong enough," he muttered. "Go. Rescue . . . your . . . friends." He took one last breath, then closed his eyes.

"Holy splarsh," Tayo said, tears in her eyes. "He's . . . he's dead! What do we do now?"

Calli blinked back a few tears of her own. "You heard what he said. We need to rescue our friends. Then his death won't have been in vain."

"That's what Vomat said about Austin and Closs being captured," Tayo said. "What's your plan?"

Calli looked around for a micro, then pointed at the closet where they had placed the sleeping Fia and Handy. They removed a large tarp from the closet and placed it over Vomat's body. They didn't want to move him for fear of spreading a trail of blood.

Then they made their way to the hall where the cells were supposed to be. Before they entered, Tayo stopped her partner. "For Vomat," she said, holding out her hand.

Calli took it. "For Vomat."

Chapter Thirty-Four

Tayo and Calli headed toward the cells with newfound determination. They had grown used to sneaking or crawling past people and were working very well as a team. At last, they reached a long hall. "There's one guard," Tayo whispered. "How do you think we should do this?"

Calli thought for a moment. "I'll go out and distract him. Then you sneak up behind him, sleeper ready."

"Let me distract him," Tayo said. "I've been praticin'. Ya know, I can talk like Roy if I wanna, and the guard is gonna believe I belong here."

"You're taller than I am," Calli said calmly. "And stronger. It will be a lot easier for you to overpower him than for me to do it. We need to act smart...we've been lucky so far. Besides, no matter what you sound like, you're still dressed like you're from Vomat's camp."

"You're right," Tayo agreed. Lesser things had turned into major arguments between them, but Tayo now viewed her partner with a new respect. "Whenever you're ready."

"Plus that accent was pathetic," Calli added with a small grin.

Calli waited until Tayo was in position behind the guard. She took a deep breath. "Excuse me," she called, just loudly enough so that only he could hear her, "do you have the time?"

The surprised guard instinctively looked at his wrist, and then back at Calli. "What are ya doin' here?" He took a couple of steps forward.

Calli positioned her own sleeper rag in her hand but

otherwise didn't move. She avoided looking at Tayo, who was right behind the guard. "Isn't it obvious? I'm here for my friends."

At that moment, Tayo reached around and placed the rag over the guard's mouth. His body went limp. Tayo caught him, Calli gave her a hand, and they pulled him around a corner. "We make a good team," Calli whispered.

Tayo smiled. "We sure do, partner."

Lawson stood in his dormitory room, staring out the window. "I just want to go home," he said. "I'm tired of all of this. I'm tired of dreaming about the Learning Center. I want to see it again."

"Listen to me, Lawson," Gren's voice pleaded, "I have good news. I found Roy. He's been searching the woods, trying to locate Calli and Tayo. I let him know they'd made contact with Vomat and Vomat's people were going to help. Roy wants us to meet him at his ship. He says the girls will know where it is."

"What's the use?" Lawson asked. "We're never going to get out of here. And Calli and Tayo are supposed to *rescue* us? Get real ...they can't even agree when to eat their morning meal."

"They're not *that* bad."

Lawson sighed. "Gren, you live with them. Do you really think those two could cooperate long enough to pull off a rescue?"

Gren's voice didn't answer. "Gren, are you still there?"

"Yes," her voice said, her smile evident even though Lawson couldn't see her. "I'm *sure* they can pull it off."

The door swung open, and Calli and Tayo rushed into the room. They threw their arms around Gren.

"How did you get here?" Gren asked at last. "There are cameras everywhere."

"We've been lucky," Calli said.

"Plus I think that most of the cameras are for show," Tayo added. "They don't really work. That's the only thing I can think of. But in case I'm wrong, we'd better hurry. Where are the boys?"

"They're all in the same place," Gren replied. "Follow me." Quietly, without being seen, they went back down the hall. "This is it," Gren whispered.

"Yeah, I can hear Sham snoring," Calli said. "I always thought Lawson was joking about that!" She typed in Fia's code. The door opened. Lawson lay on the bed; Sham and Titus were cramped on the floor. All three boys were sound asleep.

"Lawson was dreaming a micro ago," Gren said. "That's how we've been keeping in touch. I hate to think of all the rules we've broken."

"It's been under unusual circumstances," Tayo replied. "I'm sure that there are exceptions."

Careful to not break any more rules, Gren kicked the bottom of Lawson's bed. "Wake up. We need to move. Now!"

"But I just fell asleep," Lawson complained. He put his head back down, then lifted it again. "Oh, wow, this is real! I thought I was dreaming."

He bent over and shook Sham's shoulder. He then did the same for Titus. "Come on, guys, wake up. We're finally out of here."

Sham stretched and yawned, then noticed the girls standing in the doorway. "Holy . . . how did you get in here?"

"We're leaving now, Sham," Calli said. "Are you planning on coming with us?"

"Calli and Tayo are going to get us out of here, and Roy is waiting at his ship," Gren explained.

"You found Roy?" Sham asked, pulling himself to his feet. He reached down and helped Titus up. "That's good news."

"What are we waiting for? Let's go," Tayo said impatiently.

∘ ∘ ◦ ● ● ∘ ∘

The group of six students easily made it down the first hall. Calli and Tayo both glanced at the sleeping guard. They turned right. "Where are you going?" Lawson asked. "The lift is this way."

"Which is why we're taking the stairs," Calli told him. "As soon as they discover you're gone, the first place they'll check is the lift."

"And the second is the stairs," Lawson said, "which is why we should take the lift. It's faster."

"Look," Tayo started, "if you think Vomat sacrificed everything just so you could get caught again..."

"Wait a hundred," Gren interrupted. "Where *is* Vomat? And the other people you said were coming with him?"

Calli and Tayo looked at each other. "Vomat is dead," Tayo said sadly. "We think this Handy you've told us about killed him."

"Handy and Fia are both sound asleep in a storage closet," Calli added.

"The other two people with us were captured," Tayo continued. "They won't say anything about the rescue, but when we're back outside, we need to return to Vomat's camp, let them know what happened so they can send another rescue party."

"Vomat died because of us? We'll take the stairs," Lawson agreed, a hint of guilt in his voice.

Getting out of the building was easier than getting in. Calli and Tayo both averted their eyes when they passed the place where Vomat lay. They didn't mention what was under the tarp, but Gren was pretty sure she knew.

They went down the stairs, across the building to the other stairwell, and then tiptoed down the second set of stairs. A woman spotted them, but Calli and Tayo sprang into action and were soon placing her gently in a dark room.

As they entered the final, bright hallway, they passed the original guard. He was still mumbling in his sleep.

"This way," Calli instructed. They hurried down the hall, typed in Captain Fia's code one last time, and passed through the hidden doorway. They were finally outside of the building in the dirty, dusty, secret corridor.

Tayo took the light from her pocket and pointed with it. "Look, it's one of the bags we brought with us. Vomat must have decided to leave it behind for when we returned."

"Let's see what we have," Calli decided. She opened the bag and handed out food and water. Everyone took some except her partner, who was standing on the side, staring down. Calli approached her, water in hand. "Are you okay?"

"Look," Tayo said, pointing at the ground. The map that Vomat had drawn in the dust was still visible. "I feel terrible about what happened. He wanted to help us . . ."

Calli put her arm around Tayo's shoulder. "I know. I feel the same way. He was a brave, selfless man. And I realize that we didn't know him for very long, but you know what I think?" Tayo shook her head. "I think he'd be proud of us. I mean, we did it. *We did it!* "

Tayo chuckled. "Funny thing is, we talked him into bringing us along so that we could wander if necessary, but once we got inside we didn't wander at all." She took a sip of water. "I think we should probably get going."

"You're right."

The journey through the corridor took less time going back. Everyone was excited. Although they knew they still needed to find Roy and Puck, every step felt closer to home. Even the jicks they saw along the way didn't bother them. The dusty footprints helped to lead the way.

When they arrived at the entrance, they all stopped. They had a problem. Although they could reach the door, it was quite a way off the ground, too far to pull themselves up.

"We'll start with one of the guys," Calli instructed. "Sham, Titus and Lawson will boost you up. Then, once you're on the outside, we'll do it one by one. Guys first, then the girls. And don't break any rules unless we absolutely have to."

Sham was surprised by Calli's confidence and her sudden willingness to give orders, but he thought the plan made sense. Lawson and Titus lifted him up, and he pulled himself through the opening. He reached back down and grabbed hold of Titus as he came through. Last of the boys was Lawson.

The girls did the same thing, Gren first, who helped pull up Tayo. Last they reached down and pulled Calli up by her arms. Everyone stopped to catch their breath, relieved that the "no contact" rule hadn't been broken.

"Okay, long enough break," Tayo said after a hundred. "We need to head back to Vomat's camp to let them know where Austin and Closs are, Then we'll find Roy." She took off, followed by the rest of the group.

"Are you sure you know the way, Tayo?" Sham teased.

Calli wasn't in a teasing mood. "She does. We *both* do. Some of us didn't build a fire and allow ourselves to be captured..."

"Hold it right there," a voice interrupted. Everyone recognized the voice as Captain Fia's. They turned around slowly. At least twenty members of the Royal Abacuan Army were there, sticks pointed at the students.

Fia rubbed her temples and turned to Calli and Tayo. "You would be well advised to drop those sleeper rags of yours at your feet. That stuff leaves one with such a terrible headache." The Greens did as they were told. "It's a good thing we have plenty of antidote. Now please, all of you, follow me without any complaining. I am *so sick and tired* of all the complaining!"

Chapter Thirty-Five

It was a solemn group that walked through the woods. A light rain was falling steadily, contributing to the mood. Tears fell freely down Calli's face. Tayo put her arm around her partner's shoulder. "It's going to be okay," she said, trying to convince herself as well.

"They brought Gren here to wander Vomat," Calli said, trying to catch her breath. "Now he's dead. What use do they have for any of us anymore?"

"See?" Tayo said, false hope in her voice. "If they have no use for us, they'll take us home."

Several steps ahead of the Greens, Gren walked next to Lawson. It was nice to be with him, to stand next to him and walk with him like they used to, although it felt nothing like home. "What do you think is going to happen?"

Lawson sighed. "Our being here got Vomat killed. They'll probably keep us around long enough to make sure the camp is defeated, then . . . I don't know. My guess is that they'll still use us, see who else they can conquer through your abilities. They think it worked once already."

"Shhh!" Gren implored. "They don't know I wasn't really wandering him!" She stomped her foot as she walked. "If only our friends hadn't decided to play the hero and try to rescue us. Then we'd be the only two in this mess."

Sham had heard Gren's last comment. "Hey, we weren't trying to 'play the hero!' We realized you were in trouble and wanted to see what we could do to help you. We never meant for any of this to happen. Excuse us for caring."

"Sham," Gren started, "I didn't mean it that way. I appreciate your intentions, I really do. I'm just frustrated. We were so close!"

"We would have done the same thing for you, Sham," Lawson said. "You know we would have."

Sham moved closer. "We still have a chance," he whispered to Gren. "Roy is still out there. If you can wander him, then maybe he can contact Vomat's forces and they can storm the Headquarters or something."

"They'd probably be willing to help," Titus added. "After all, two of their members are already inside, and Handy did kill their leader."

A small amount of hope raced through Gren's body. "Keep squabbling," she said. "If they think we're mad at each other, they won't know we're forming a plan. I'll let Calli and Tayo know."

"Squabbling?" Sham repeated.

Half a unit later, the group stood outside Headquarters. Captain Fia went to the front of the group and punched in her new code; the door opened. Everyone, including the twenty army members, followed her inside. Instead of heading toward the lift, she walked through the lobby and across the building. At another door, she entered her code again and led them all through.

They entered a large room, larger than any other room they had seen within the building. There were rows and rows of seats, and an open area in the front. "It's a theater!" Gren said.

"Ah, Gren, there's no fooling you," Fia replied, a smile on her face. She turned so she could see the entire group. "I want the students to sit in the front with their partners; everyone else can fill in the rows behind them."

Confused, the six students took their seats. The seats directly behind them were soon filled, the stick weapons still in the guards' hands. Other people filed in, as well...talking, laughing, seeming to have a good time. Gren ignored them and immediately tried to reach out to Roy, hoping he was asleep or at least letting his mind wander. She knew it was a long shot, but it was the only shot they had.

Several empty chairs waited on the stage. Handy walked up the stairs and sat down. Fia followed him onto the stage, but instead of sitting she spoke with someone on the side. She disappeared into the wings.

More people entered; the theater was quickly filled. The lights in the theater went out, and some loud music played. An amplified male voice filled the room: "Ladies, gentlemen, and Dream Wandering students, the Royal Abacuan Theater is proud to present . . . Captain Fia in *Lessons Learned!*"

Those sitting behind the students cheered. A spotlight shone on the stage and Fia came out, holding a microphone.

"Thank you, thank you. A bit overly dramatic, to be sure, but after what we've put these six through, it's time to have some fun. Before we start with the explanations, I'd like to introduce just a few of the people who have made this possible. First, Handy."

The stage lights came up. Handy stood and waved, accepting the applause.

"Next, two gentlemen we've really enjoyed having around... Austin and Closs!"

The pair walked onto the stage, waved to the clapping audience, and took their seats next to Handy.

"Another true gentleman, one without whose help we wouldn't have been able to pull this off, please welcome Roy!"

The applause grew.

"There goes our plan," Lawson whispered to Gren as Roy took his seat. "Looks like Roy has been captured, as well."

"He's obviously playing along with whatever they're doing," Gren answered. "The other two, as well. Maybe we'll all be able to make a break for it."

"Keep an eye on the stick weapons," Lawson suggested. "Maybe in the dark we can grab a couple. I'll tell Sham, you tell Calli."

Before Gren could repeat what Lawson had told her, Fia continued. "Here's someone I know the two Greens will be happy to see. As the commander of the opposition, put your hands together for Vomat!"

Calli screamed, "What?"

Vomat, clothes covered in red, but very much alive, walked onto the stage and took his seat next to Roy.

Fia laughed. "Calli, is it?" Calli nodded. "Calli, dear, please. Not in the middle of the introductions. Nobody likes a heckler." The rest of the audience laughed. Fia held up a hand to quiet them.

"Now, as you can see, there are three seats left. One, of course, is mine, and I'm pretty happy about it, because I get to sit between two incredibly handsome men." There was more laughter. Fia smiled. "That wasn't a joke," she informed the crowd, although there was a chuckle in her voice. "The other two seats . . . Well, let me just say that it is quite an honor to introduce these two people. Two people I admire and respect. One of them I've known well since I was a White in the Dream Wandering program.

"A micro for some background: I was released from that program after several orbits, and I'm glad I was, because otherwise I wouldn't have ended up here. But back to my introductions. This man and I have remained friends over the orbits. The other person who is about to join us . . . Well, let's just say that I have more respect for her than for most people I've met. I'm so glad that, once again, we've had the chance to work with these two and help them out. All the way from the Dream Wandering Learning Center; I am absolutely thrilled to introduce Hutch and Ladinda!"

The applause was almost deafening. The only people not cheering were the six students seated in the front row. Hutch came out first, gave Fia a hug, and took a seat, leaving an empty space between his chair and Vomat's. Ladinda followed, walking to the center of the stage. She bowed, obviously enjoying the attention. Fia handed her the microphone and took her seat between Hutch and Vomat.

"Thank you so much, you're too kind." Ladinda glanced back at the chairs. Handy jumped up, grabbed the empty chair on the end, and pulled it to the front of the stage. "Thank you, Handy," she said, sitting down.

From her new seat she could see her six students, but not clearly. "Could we bring up the house lights a little bit? I'd really like to be able to see their faces as they find out what has really been going on."

Chapter Thirty-Six

Ladinda seemed to take forever making herself comfortable. She waited until the lights were at an acceptable level, crossed her legs, cleared her throat, and then leaned forward slightly.

"I know that all six of you have a million questions running through your minds. There will be time to ask...not only of me, but of any of us. First, though, let me assure you that you were never in any danger. Now, I want you to close your eyes and think back to when you were Whites. On Partnering Rotation I give a speech. Every time, it's pretty much the same thing, so you've heard it every orbit. Now, open your eyes. What is one thing I always mention?"

Sham raised his hand. "No classes?"

The entire auditorium laughed. Ladinda smiled. "That's true, I do mention that, but that's not what I'm looking for. Anyone else?"

"Dream wandering without permission is against the law?" Calli tried.

"That's very good, Calli," Ladinda said. "That's actually part of what this has been about, but it's bigger than that." She looked at Gren. "You know what I'm talking about. I know you do."

Gren nodded. "'A journey that will be filled with many trials, tests, and tribulations, but a journey that is indeed worth taking,'" she recited.

"Exactly!" Ladinda exclaimed. "That's what this has been...a test. Your outburst, Lawson, when you wandered Dod's dream, came at the perfect time. Everything had already been set up, but you made it more believable. The timing was perfect for the lesson you needed to learn."

"You wanted to show me that I needed to take things more seriously," Lawson said, the revelation obvious in his voice.

"That is indeed a very large part of it," Ladinda agreed. "You see, Lawson, you have a gift, a gift that is also a responsibility. I knew you'd joked about becoming . . ." she glanced at Hutch. "What did he call it?"

"'A wandering Dream Wanderer,'" Hutch replied, raising his voice enough so everyone could hear.

Ladinda shook her head. "Not good. So part of this exercise was to show you exactly why wandering is allowed only under controlled situations, and only with permission. The laws are there for a reason. And I must say that, Gren, you have made me very proud. You broke no laws. A few minor rules, perhaps, but that was to be expected. Yours talents are remarkable...you indeed have a potential that even most of our teachers can only dream of. With the right apprenticeship you will be able to do so much good with your abilities."

She smiled again. "And I must comment that there is one rule, which I know neither you nor Lawson is particularly fond of, that you still didn't break. I am extremely pleased with both of you for that."

Gren and Lawson exchanged glances, knowing that Ladinda was speaking of the "no contact with students of the opposite gender" rule.

Tayo raised her hand. "I have a question. You say we weren't in any danger, but what about those weapons?"

"May I see one, please?" Ladinda asked. Handy handed his to her. "Thank you. It was all an illusion. The special effects department rigged a couple of them to make you think they were dangerous, but in reality..." Ladinda pressed the button that everyone thought fired the weapon. There was only a small puff of smoke. "That's all that happens. It's a prop, not much more than a child's toy. There was an explosion or two rigged to *look* like they'd come from the stick but, as I said, it was just a special effect. Granted, some threats were made, and I am truly sorry that those were necessary, but they were all part of the test."

Titus raised his hand. "Special effects department? Just where are we?"

Ladinda motioned to Fia. "I'll let you handle this one."

Fia came forward and took the microphone from Ladinda. "We're on Abacu, just as we said. But not the planet." She laughed. "Everyone knows there's no life on other planets." The audience laughed, as well. "Abacu is also the name of an island on the far side of Terra. It's home to two different industries: the Science Center and the Arts and Entertainment Department. That's where we are right now.

"We sometimes help out the various Learning Centers with different projects, when someone needs to learn a lesson. Ladinda came to me at the beginning of the current orbit, and this plan has been in the works ever since. Most of us here, including the audience, are actors." She looked out at the sea of people. "Give yourselves a round of applause; we really pulled this one off!" The audience roared with pleasure.

Fia quieted them when she saw Sham's hand up. "Sham, did you have a question?"

"I don't know," he stammered. He seemed upset. "Roy, you told me you were from outer space!"

Roy stood up and took the microphone from Fia. "No," he

said, "ya *assumed* I was from outer space. I told ya I was from Abacu. I am. I grew up at the Science Center and worked there until my wife got sick." He looked at Calli. "That part of it was true. Breeze *was* exposed to a fatal gas. We flew to the other side of the planet because the air was better. That's where she died, and that's where I made my new home."

"But if we're still on Terra, how did we get here?" Sham asked.

"Puck really is mine," Roy told him. "She's a model that I was workin' on in my spare time when Breeze had her accident. I took Puck with me. I've been workin' on the modifications ever since. So when ya came to me, we took her out, far enough into space so ya could get a feel for it, then turned around and headed here. The dark cloud ya saw before we landed was real. It's a byproduct of the Science Center, although it's perfectly harmless."

"What about the space walk we took?" Sham asked.

Roy grinned. "*That* was real."

Fia took the microphone. "The Science Center loaned us a ship, as well...one they've been working on for deep space exploration. We did the same thing Roy did: flew out a bit, then turned around and came back. The pilots and crew all work at the Science Center. And we divided our actors into two main groups, based on their accents. Those who were from this area became part of the army. Those who are from an area a couple of units away became part of Vomat's camp. Those who don't do either accent well just kept their mouths shut."

"What about the symbol?" Titus wanted to know.

"Yeah," Sham said, "I remember seeing that when I was a kid!"

"I knew ya would," Roy said, after taking back the

microphone. "That symbol is for the Science Center. When Ladinda first approached me about doin' all this, I showed it to her, knowin' that ya would remember it. I'm no actor...I was a bit worried about my part, so they said anythin' that was real would help me get better into character. I basically played myself, but instead of that symbol meanin' the Science Center, we changed it to the Royal Abacuan Army."

"The costume department had a lot of fun with it," Fia added, leaning into the microphone.

"And Handy really is my cousin," Roy informed them.

"What if we hadn't contacted Roy?" Sham asked.

Ladinda held out her hand, and Roy gave her back the microphone. "Then he would have run into you and asked what was wrong. But we knew how close you all are, and we knew that you would do anything you could to help your friends. I must say I was a bit disappointed in Lanna and Macy; I thought they would want to help, as well. Friendship is a valuable gift, and having people who would do anything for you is priceless."

She looked down the row of students. "Who has the next question?"

Tayo held up her hand. "If we're still on Terra, why did it take so long to get here?"

"Some things shouldn't be rushed," Ladinda replied. "This needed to be a lesson that you would never forget. I also thought the test would be better if it was learned after the initial fear of the situation had started to subside. It was easier to learn if some boredom was allowed to set in. Now, are there any more questions?"

"I have one," Lawson said. "Handy mentioned to Gren and me that the gravity was different on Abacu, and it really felt different. So how . . ."

"The power of suggestion," Ladinda told him. "We thought you would be more likely to believe you were no longer on Terra if we placed a suggestion or two in your minds. The gravity on both ships was raised slightly, then slowly readjusted before landing. It was just a little mind game. Anyone else?"

Tayo raised her hand. "What about Vomat? He was dead!"

"And his dream was so real," Gren added.

Ladinda looked back at Vomat, who stood up and took the microphone. "The dream was also because of the power of suggestion. I had made up a story about a ship being shot down and continued to replay it in my mind after I took the sleep tonic. I am glad it worked, because it is hard to control what one dreams. And my 'death' was all planned out as well. Let me assure you, it was fake blood. I was worried you would try to take my pulse; that was the one thing I had no control over. I tried to keep you from doing that with my death scene." He grinned from ear to ear. "A good death scene is every actor's dream. My character needed to die, because it was not up to me to rescue Gren and Lawson. It was up to the two of you, Tayo and Calli."

"Why us?" Calli asked.

Ladinda smiled as she reclaimed the microphone. "I would think *that* was obvious. You see, my dears, this was your lesson, as well."

"Ours?" Calli and Tayo asked in unison.

"Look at the two of you," Ladinda said. "You've *both* been through several partners, you were *both* close to being released from the program, but you *both* have so much potential. For some reason, you couldn't get along. I know it was a bit drastic, but we needed to do something to force you to work together and, more importantly, to show you that, given a chance, you might discover you actually like each other."

Calli looked at Tayo, then back at Ladinda. "You're right, I *do* like her. I think I was just so scared of changing partners again that I tried to force her away."

"I don't think we have to worry about that anymore," Tayo said. She too looked at Ladinda. "Thank you."

Ladinda stood up. "I think we're just about done here. Roy will take you back home; it should only take a few units. If you have any more questions I'm sure he'll be pleased to answer them."

"Wait, just one more thing," Gren pleaded. "Our parents, the other students, the system workers..."

Ladinda held up a hand. "That's all been taken care of. Your parents gave their permission...all except Lawson's, of course, but as head of the Learning Center I'm his official guardian. The rest of your parents know all about it. Those weren't real system workers; they were also actors. In fact, they're here right now. Where are the 'system workers' seated?"

A group cheer came from the back of the theater. Everyone turned around as several people waved.

"You obviously were very convincing," Ladinda said. "Now, back to Gren's question. When the break is over, the other students will be informed that it was all a misunderstanding; neither Lawson nor Gren had anything to do with the missing sleep tonic. The official reason you weren't at school that last rotation was that Gren's parents had picked you up early for the break. I found the note from your parents after the assembly that rotation."

Ladinda's face grew serious. "One very important new rule for the six of you: You must not speak of this to any of the other students. Remember, we have another girl/boy partnering, and those two remind me very much of Gren and Lawson. Although it's been several orbits since the last time we did this, we might have to arrange more 'trials, tests and tribulations.' So it's very important for whoever is next to think it's real."

"What about Lanna and Macy?" Gren wanted to know. "Can we tell them?"

Ladinda shook her head. "They had their chance to be a part of it, but they decided instead to play it safe. They will be assigned to a new room so that you three can speak freely of these events in private."

Ladinda faced the audience. "I think we're just about done. Thank you once again for your help in this matter. I hope that everyone enjoyed this role-playing game."

Soon the applause died down, the stage lights faded, and the house lights were raised. It was over.

Chapter Thirty-Seven

Graduation Rotation was the biggest celebration of the orbit. Color by color, the students came in and took their seats. A new robe, the color of next orbit's uniform, was waiting for them. Angel and Dod were the first two to enter; they had made it through their first orbit as partners. There were always fewer students at graduation than on Partnering Rotation; each orbit, some did not make it. Those who had were filled with the satisfaction of being one step closer to becoming licensed Dream Wanderers. The Blues were the last to enter; they took their seats on the stage.

After everyone was seated, Ladinda took her place in the front. "I promise, I will keep this short," she said. "This had been a fantastic orbit, one of the best I can remember...and I've been here a long time. Yes, there have been problems, misunderstandings, trials, tests, and tribulations, but I think you've all grown stronger for it.

"I see the Blues seated here with me. I am so proud of this class. They have proved to me that they are strong, capable, and moral. I look at the Greens, knowing they have just one more orbit. They have grown in so many ways, not just physically, but in maturity. I am sure that, next orbit, they will prove more than capable of becoming the leaders I expect them to be. Then there are the Yellows . . ."

Gren tried to concentrate on Ladinda's speech but found it hard. Yes, the Greens had matured; two of them in ways that few people knew about. Calli and Tayo had become so close that at times it had been hard sharing a room with them; Gren often felt left out.

The Blues . . . she knew that part of Ladinda's monologue had been directed at her. Under what she had thought were the worst of circumstances, she hadn't broken the moral code of the Dream Wanderers. She knew that her future was going to be even better; she was about to become an apprentice to one of the top Dream Wanderers in the business. Lawson had accepted a position there, as well. The firm didn't normally take apprentices, but both had received personal invitations on Ladinda's recommendation. Sham and Titus would be with a different group not far away. None of them would be more than two units away from the Learning Center, so it would be easy to visit Calli and Tayo.

From where she was sitting, Gren could see the invited guests. Her parents were near the front with her little sister, Winnie. She could see her friends' families, as well. In the back row was an unusual group. Vomat sat on the end, next to Closs, Austin, Roy, Handy, and Fia. Gren had been surprised to learn that Fia had told the truth: she and Hutch had, at one time, been partnered. The smiles on their faces showed they were happy to be there, proud to have played a part in bringing this strange group to the point of graduation.

The spectators' applause told Gren Ladinda's speech was over. Along with the other Blues, she stood. Two by two, Ladinda called their names. Partners stepped forward, accepted the multi-colored robe offered by Hutch or Charla, then shook Ladinda's hand. They then stood on the other side of the stage, proud graduates of the program. Most of the group had already been called when Sham and Titus's names were spoken. They stepped forward and proudly accepted their graduation robes.

Ladinda paused before she called the final two names. "I

have saved this partnering for last on purpose. Some of you may not realize this, but these two have been together since Partnering Rotation when they were Whites. It's the first time in the history of the Learning Center that a boy/girl partnering has made it through the entire program. With a great sense of pride, I call forth Gren and Lawson."

The audience stood as Gren accepted her robe from Charla and Lawson took his from Hutch. There were tears in Gren's eyes as she shook Ladinda's hand. "Thank you," Gren whispered, "for everything."

· ₀₀●₀₀ ₀

The celebration after the ceremony was filled with joy. The younger students had put on their new robes, signifying their next rotation. Most students joined their families or were busy saying goodbye to friends. Sham and Titus threw a ball back and forth. Calli and Tayo, dressed in blue robes, were huddled together, making plans for the break. Although Gren was with her family, Lawson approached her. "Do you have a hundred that you could spare for your former partner?" he asked.

"Anything for you," Gren replied with a smile. She and Lawson walked silently toward the lake.

"I'm going to miss this place," Lawson said at last.

"Me, too."

"I can't believe we finally graduated! We did it, Gren, we really did it."

"So much is changing." Gren wiped away a tear from the corner of her eye.

"I know," Lawson said. "But for the better. For example, now that we're *former* students...I can finally do this." Lawson pulled Gren into a hug, an embrace that was long overdue. For the first time since they had known each other, Gren didn't resist.

Epilogue

As the ride came to a stop Gren looked around her. Lawson was seated next to her with a puzzled look on his face. "That was some ride," he said at last.

"Yeah," was all that Gren could say. She had no idea what had really happened or if Lawson had experienced the same thing that she had just been through. She didn't want to ask him for fear that she would sound like she was crazy.

The two of them took a few steps forward and into the gift shop at the exit of the ride. They stood there for a moment, trying to get their bearings. "Wild ride, isn't it?" Gren knew without looking that Roy was standing next to them. "Did ya have a good time?"

"The best," Lawson replied.

"Ya better hurry, Gren," Roy said. "I don't want ya to be late meeting your parents. And Lawson, ya need to meet up with your group as well."

Gren glanced at her watch. Although it felt like she had been gone for months, it was only 25 minutes since the last time that she had checked it. "I'd better go."

"Wait," Lawson said quickly. "I don't want to lose touch," he lowered his voice, "especially after all that we've been through."

"So it really did happen," Gren mumbled. She looked up. "I'm not supposed to give people I don't know my cell phone number."

"The two of ya aren't exactly strangers anymore," Roy said.

"True." Gren pulled out her cell phone and handed it to Lawson. "You can put your number in, if you want to."

Lawson smiled as he took Gren's phone and added his number. "Text me yours."

"I will. I really need to get going. Roy, thanks for...where did he go?"

"I don't know. Maybe he was all a dream."

Gren decided to take a chance to see Lawson's reaction. She still wasn't sure what had happened during the ride. "And we also dreamed up Tayo, Calli, Titus, and Sham?"

"The first three maybe," Lawson replied. "But I don't think that even with my imagination that I could dream up someone like Sham."

Gren and Lawson left the store together, talking about their adventure. They did not know how it had happened, they just knew that something did take place. They promised to keep in touch and then Gren walked off to find her family.

"Over here!" Winnie was jumping up and down, waving her arms. "We're over here Gren!"

Gren was smiling as she approached her family. "Did you get the picture?"

"It was so much fun, Gren!" Winnie replied. "When we told Pooh my name he laughed and gave me a great big hug! How was the ride?"

"Intense," Gren replied.

"You're still too little," their mother said quickly. "I wouldn't want you to have nightmares from it, Winnie."

"But Mom..."

"Mom is right," Gren said quickly. "You need to work your way up to it. But next year, little sister, you're definitely riding with me!"

Title: *Dream Wanderers Apprentices*
- Author: Paula Brown
- Publisher: Mouse Gate Press
- Paper Back: ISBN: 9781590957929
- eBook: ISBN: 9781590957936
- Number of pages 240
- Publication Date: August 16, 2016

A visit from Gren's little sister and a friend turns dangerous because of a case of mistaken identity; and it is up to Gren and her friends to use their talents and find the girl before it's too late.

Gren is excited because her little sister Winnie and Winnie's friend Mollie are going to spend their school break with her. Gren's friends Calli and Tayo agree to spend their break with her as well, to help take care of the children while Gren is at work. What Gren doesn't know is that Mollie has a problem that she wants assistance with; her dreams come true. Someone learns of Mollie's ability to see the future and sets a plan in motion to kidnap her and profit from her gift. What the person doesn't realize is that Winnie was grabbed instead. Gren and her friends use their skills to try to find Winnie, before the kidnapper realizes the mistake.